SECOND CHANCE REUNION

Sunset SEALs Book 6

SHARON HAMILTON

SHARON HAMILTON'S BOOK LIST

SEAL BROTHERHOOD BOOKS

SEAL BROTHERHOOD SERIES
Accidental SEAL Book 1
Fallen SEAL Legacy Book 2
SEAL Under Covers Book 3
SEAL The Deal Book 4
Cruisin' For A SEAL Book 5
SEAL My Destiny Book 6
SEAL of My Heart Book 7
Fredo's Dream Book 8
SEAL My Love Book 9
SEAL Encounter Prequel to Book 1
SEAL Endeavor Prequel to Book 2
Ultimate SEAL Collection Vol. 1 Books 1-4 /2 Prequels
Ultimate SEAL Collection Vol. 2 Books 5-7

SEAL BROTHERHOOD LEGACY SERIES
Watery Grave Book 1
Honor The Fallen Book 2
Grave Injustice Book 3
Deal With The Devil Book 4

BAD BOYS OF SEAL TEAM 3 SERIES
SEAL's Promise Book 1
SEAL My Home Book 2
SEAL's Code Book 3
Big Bad Boys Bundle Books 1-3

Sunset SEALs Duet #2

LOVE VIXEN
Bone Frog Love

SHADOW SEALS
Shadow of the Heart
Shadow Warrior

SILVER SEALS SERIES
SEAL Love's Legacy

SLEEPER SEALS SERIES
Bachelor SEAL

STAND ALONE BOOKS & SERIES
SEAL's Goal: The Beautiful Game
Nashville SEAL: Jameson
True Blue SEALS Zak
Paradise: In Search of Love
Love Me Tender, Love You Hard

NOVELLAS
SEAL You In My Dreams Magnolias and Moonshine

PARANORMALS

GOLDEN VAMPIRES OF TUSCANY SERIES
Honeymoon Bite Book 1
Mortal Bite Book 2
Christmas Bite Book 3
Midnight Bite Book 4

THE GUARDIANS
Heavenly Lover Book 1
Underworld Lover Book 2
Underworld Queen Book 3
Redemption Book 4

FALL FROM GRACE SERIES
Gideon: Heavenly Fall

NOVELLAS
SEAL Of Time Trident Legacy

All of Sharon's books are available on Audible,
narrated by the talented J.D. Hart.

This is a work of fiction. Names, characters, places, brands, media, and incidents are either the product of the author's imagination or are used fictitiously. In many cases, liberties and intentional inaccuracies have been taken with rank, description of duties, locations and aspects of the SEAL community.

ABOUT THE BOOK

A baby given up for adoption…
This second chance couple learns the true meaning of Family…
Like the Brotherhood…no one gets left behind.

As the daughter they gave up for adoption 12 years ago comes back into their lives, Damon and Martel plan their June wedding and Martel's move to San Diego.

But this new second chance has a rocky start with ST3's disappointing mission to Mexico Damon is held responsible for.

Martel struggles with giving up a job and house she loves at the beach in Florida for an unknown future in Coronado with her fiance's career hanging in the balance.

Do they have the grit to keep it tight when enemies keep springing up at every turn?

AUTHOR'S NOTE

I always dedicate my SEAL Brotherhood books to the brave men and women who defend our shores and keep us safe. Without their sacrifice, and that of their families—because a warrior's fight always includes his or her family—I wouldn't have the freedom and opportunity to make a living writing these stories. They sometimes pay the ultimate price so we can debate, argue, go have coffee with friends, raise our children and see them have children of their own.

One of my favorite tributes to warriors resides on many memorials, including one I saw honoring the fallen of WWII on an island in the Pacific:

> "When you go home
> Tell them of us, and say
> For your tomorrow,
> We gave our today."

These are my stories created out of my own imagination. Anything that is inaccurately portrayed is either my mistake, or done intentionally to disguise something I might have overheard over a beer or in the corner of one of the hangouts along the Coronado Strand.

I support two main charities. Navy SEAL/UDT Museum operates in Ft. Pierce, Florida. Please learn about this wonderful museum, all run by active and former SEALs and their friends and families, and who rely on public support, not that of the U.S. Government. www.navysealmuseum.org

I also support Wounded Warriors, who tirelessly bring together the warrior as well as the family members who are just learning to deal with their soldier's condition and have nowhere to turn. It is a long path to becoming well, but I've seen first-hand what this organization does for its warriors and the families who love them. Please give what your heart tells you is right. If you cannot give, volunteer at one of the many service centers all over the United States. Get involved. Do something meaningful for someone who gave so much of themselves, to families who have paid the price for your freedom. You'll find a family there unlike any other on the planet. www.woundedwarriorproject.org

CHAPTER 1

Friday before Valentine's Weekend

D AMON HAMLIN STEWED over what to get Martel for Valentine's Day. They'd been apart for a month, and she'd be flying in to visit him for Valentine's Day, but she'd only be here that one day. Engaged, they planned on a June beach wedding, most of which she was handling. Not to mention, she needed to finish out the school year in Florida, saying goodbye to her parents and other teachers he knew she loved.

Because she was going to come live with him in San Diego, she was giving up her little house at Sunset Beach. And he worried it was perhaps asking too much.

What did she have to do to convince him she was actually joining him in San Diego? He wondered why he doubted things all of a sudden. Maybe it was because the next day after their night of romance, she intended to visit their daughter in Palo Alto—the baby she'd given up for adoption while he was off being a Boy Scout on his SEAL Team 3. Even though he didn't know about her until this year, he felt he should have known. He should have done a lot of things differently.

He'd made so many mistakes. *They'd* made a lot of mistakes together. But he still knew that Ainsley, their daughter, wasn't one of them. He would forever be grateful Martel decided to give her up for adoption rather than terminating the pregnancy—a decision she'd borne on her own. Strong, dedicated, and thinking straight, she could always be counted on to do the right thing. So he shouldn't worry or question her agreement to marry him, to give them a second chance to have that happily ever after, even though they'd blown the first one so badly.

Maybe it worried him that he wasn't worth what she trusted or saw in him. It was sort of imposter syndrome. Would she find out in time that he really wasn't the honorable man she thought him to be? He had been so weak and uncaring, so selfish, thinking the whole world revolved around him. He liked to tell himself it was because he had to focus on his demanding job—demanding emotionally as well as physically.

But that was a lie, because the job fit his limited capacity to think emotionally and deeply. It made him wonder if he ever would deserve her.

But she believed in him. That was for sure. He hoped to God he didn't disappoint her. He'd hurt her enough. She wasn't a fragile, breakable doll—she'd proven that overwhelmingly. She was strong. She loved strong. She never gave up, even when he did.

But she deserves more, doesn't she?

He couldn't tell her that he wished she'd spend all her time with him. He couldn't tell her he wished he could go with her to see their daughter. No, he had to earn that right. One thing at a time. What if the meeting caused her pain, so much pain that she didn't want to see his face again because it reminded her of the heavy decision she'd made twelve years ago? He knew it was going to be both good and hard for her at the same time.

And, God help him, he wouldn't be there to hold her hand. He'd be a phone call away while she boarded the plane and flew home to Florida to face the end of the school year all by herself. He should be there, but he couldn't be. He'd be on deployment.

Everything about his job had changed since he met her at that wedding in Florida. That second chance meeting where she just appeared, like magic—out of thin air, back into his life, and then soon back into his arms. He didn't even recognize her at first.

"What the fuck's the matter with you?" Calvin "Coop" Cooper asked him, slapping him on the back.

"I'm sorry?" He reared his head up to stare at the tall SEAL blocking the sun. The huge Adonis medic on their team had just taken one of his five-mile swims in the bay. He was just as ripped at thirty as he probably had been as a tadpole who nearly made the United States Olympic Swim Team.

"You look like you either ate too many of the Scupper pancakes or some bad seafood. Maybe something from the bottom of his chowder pot."

"That bad?" He sneered up at Coop.

The tall operator, almost the fastest swimmer on the entire platoon with hands that could palm a basketball no problem, hunkered down beside him and shook his head, as if to say, "clean up that brain of yours," and let him eat the consequences of being covered in droplets of salty bay water.

Well, he had it coming.

"I heard Martel was coming out tomorrow. You don't look like a man who's especially excited. I mean, if you were like Libby or one of the ladies, you'd be waxing yourself all over and getting a proper haircut and shave."

"Wouldn't do any good. It would grow back before tomorrow, Coop. You're the same way."

Coop rubbed the pelt on top of his head he called his hair, now beginning to thin. Soon, he'd have more hair on his chest and arms than on top. "That's probably true."

One of the things he loved the best about his SEAL buds was that they didn't have to talk much. There was this thing about syncing. Just sitting down next to a guy, and he could sort of tell what was going on. Lots of non-verbal communication.

Or maybe it was all horseshit. Damon chuckled.

"That's what I was looking for. You must be thinking about all the things you're going to do when she gets here. That's more like it."

"As a matter of fact, I was," he lied. But it was the game they played. It made no difference if it was bullshit or the truth. The rule was no lying to the women. The men, well, they could handle it, as long as it didn't put one of them in danger. Also, no lying about acting like a pussy or trying to get out of a deserved punishment. The only time SEALs lied to the women was if one of the wives asked if her husband was being unfaithful, and then no question, you had to lie. Every time. Not just sometimes, every time.

"As an older man married now nearly ten years, with three kids to chase around and a pretty wife who still looks hot in a bathing suit, I ask that you indulge me in your plans. Maybe I can learn something from your younger ones," Coop said with a big grin.

He asked not because he wanted to know, but because he wanted Damon to go there, hang around, remember who he was and what he had to do, and to stop moping and worrying about everything in the world he had no control over.

So he'd take a stab at it.

"I don't know what to get her for Valentine's Day."

"Roses are nice."

"Yeah. I thought about that."

"Hard to go wrong with those."

He wondered why the idea didn't make him feel better. Maybe it was the romance he didn't feel he deserved. Or was he looking for something special? A band-aid on the chasm he'd created and now was repairing. The truth was, he felt like he wanted to apologize to her all the time. He couldn't help it.

"You know it's normal for engaged SEALs to go a little crazy from time to time. They start imagining things. It's one thing to earn your Trident and another altogether to step up to an altar and in front of every-one say, 'I do.'" Coop gave him a long look to make sure Damon got the message, like he'd stuck a pin with that note to his forehead.

"I'm not having cold feet." Fuck it. He was about to go deep, and he couldn't help it. "I don't think I deserve her. I've done so many shitty—"

"You shut the fuck up, Damon, or you'll be single for your natural life—or until some round gets you when you're thinking that. That doesn't do any good for anybody. Besides, it ain't up to you. It's the woman who chooses."

That was true enough.

"And Martel chose you, Damon. You're it. Now is not the time to consider some other story. You should have thought about that before you—"

"Don't bring it up." He really didn't want to hear that part.

"Oh, I didn't mean—" Coop shook his head. "Fuck, I must be losing it. I didn't mean the kid, Damon. I meant before you let her fall in love with you again. You had a choice in that. But once you opened that door and let her in, she tagged you. There's no getting around it. You're it. You got no more rights, man. It's chapel time, my friend. Has nothing to do with whether or not you deserve it. It's what she wants. And knowing Martel, she'll have it too."

"So now you see my problem."

"Ain't no problem, bro. You're screwed. Lovingly screwed. Grin and enjoy the ride."

"But there's a third person in our family I keep thinking about. I think about her all the time."

That shut Coop up. He cautiously continued. "Well, I haven't had that to deal with, that I know of, anyway. You made the mistake, the both of you made the mistake, but she wasn't one of them."

"That's what Martel says too."

"And that's the right way to look at it. You two should have been together, and you blew it. Now you do the rest of your life differently. You're playing a different game."

"So back to my original thoughts. What the fuck do I get her for Valentine's Day? Besides what I've already given her, I mean."

"You just give her everything you got. You let her know how special she is. Don't go wallowing around in that self-pity crap, Damon. She doesn't find that very sexy or attractive. I don't have to tell you that."

Damon agreed. But even if he plastered the road to his condo with rose petals a foot thick, it still wasn't enough.

"Do you write?" Coop asked.

"Not really."

"Draw?"

"Nope."

"Can you tell her a story?"

"I don't like to tell stories."

"So read her something. Ever heard of Rumi? He wrote some classic love poems. Libby has several books with them. Want me to ask her?"

"No, I can do the research. That's a nice thought, though. Do you think I should get a nice room at the Hotel Del?"

"Sure, if you can get one. Women like that. But it's

going to cost you, if it's available. Valentine's is pretty big there."

"You're probably right."

"God, if I still had the Babemobile, I'd let you borrow that. Simple, just a big bed and a galley kitchen and a head."

"And more of your DNA in it than anything else in the world. No, thanks. That wouldn't work, Coop. What are you doing, trying to get me divorced before the wedding?" He was laughing now, at Coop's expense.

But the big-hearted man of steel was laughing too.

"Talk about pasts. See, I wasn't so bright, was I?"

"It worked out, though."

"As it will for you, son," he said as he put his arm around Damon's shoulders. "Can I buy you breakfast? I'm starved."

Well, he wasn't any closer to deciding what to get Martel for Valentine's Day, but the idea of a hearty breakfast with some decent coffee sounded perfect right now.

"Coop, you know just the right thing to say, don't you?" Damon said as they scrambled to their feet.

"I try. Goddammit, I try."

CHAPTER 2

MARTEL WAITED FOR the parents of one of her students. Her shared office seemed a little cramped and small today due to the clutter of papers and reference books she and her office mate and best friend, Kaitlyn, had collected over the school year. It was going to be a task to extricate herself from this little den where she had shared so much with Kate—the person she came to visit some six years ago and part of the reason she stayed in Florida, abandoning her California roots.

The space was filled with as many memories as papers and books.

This would be the last year she would be teaching here. It was the end of a long and enjoyable partnership with Kaitlyn. Combined, the two of them were the most popular teachers at the school. A part of her wanted to stay forever here, but her sensible, forward-thinking part knew she belonged in San Diego with

Damon and the new life they would be restarting there.

At least, that's what she told herself. It was a day-by-day thing. Leaving the Gulf beach community sometimes felt like she was giving up something too precious to be able to recover from—but she'd done that already and survived. If she told herself this over and over again, eventually she'd not have those doubts. But sometimes it still felt like jumping from the skydiving plane into the blue unknown that beautiful day with Damon, flying through the sky in tandem with his careful guidance then coming to a safe landing. She hoped it would turn out that way. But often, hope needed help.

Tomorrow morning, she'd be off to San Diego to spend Valentine's Day with Damon, and then she'd fly to Palo Alto the day after to visit their daughter for the first time. She was excited, nervous, and now irritated as she tapped her fingers on the folder she'd prepared for the parent-teacher conference.

Often, she would meet with parents in the classroom, but in this instance, she needed the privacy of the office where she could close the door. The discussion she needed to have with the parents had to be in private due to the nature of the meeting. These talks weren't what she had expected when she got her teaching credential. She wasn't basking in the happy, fresh-faced adoring gazes from a room full of active young minds full of life and soaking up her every word. That was the part of teaching she loved.

This was the hard part. The part no teacher ever wanted to have.

A full twenty minutes late, the young couple appeared in her doorway. Mrs. Gibbs wore cut-off jeans a little too short for her hefty legs and a halter top because it was a warm day in February. Mr. Gibbs wore a dirty light green tee shirt with a construction logo on it and jeans equally as soiled. Even his hands were stained as he extended for the obligatory shake. The mother just sat down in the chair and asked Martel if she could smoke.

"I'm sorry, no. The whole campus is non-smoking, Mrs. Gibbs."

The young mother rolled her dirty blonde head back and forth, the French braid the only part of her appearance done with care. Martel immediately had a bad feeling about the outcome of the discussion she needed to have.

"So I have some concerning news, and I want to let you know that I have not spoken to the administrator about this yet, but I intend to. And based on our discussion here this afternoon, I may be speaking to other authorities as well."

"About what?" Mrs. Gibbs barked. Her frown was ugly. Her skin was over-baked from the sun and lined before her years. She was missing two teeth on her upper right side. She would have been pretty if she'd taken a little more care, Martel noted.

Mr. Gibbs sat stoically like he was about to get hit by a train.

"I think your daughter is exhibiting behavior I've seen before in young preteens who have experienced some kind of sexual abuse, and I—"

Mrs. Gibbs was on her feet. "No way, missy. You don't give me that crap. We may be poor, but we're good people. We don't abuse our children."

Martel knew they had five at home all under the age of ten. Her student, Cora, was their eldest.

"I didn't say you abuse your children, Mrs. Gibbs. Now, would you like to sit down, or should we move this discussion to the administrator's office?"

The young mother dutifully sat, her steely eyes struggling with thoughts Martel knew she didn't want to have. She and her husband avoided each other's attention.

"Let me explain. And then, maybe, the three of us can figure out what our next step is. First, I'm required by law to report anything I see that could be viewed as abuse to higher authorities. I'm sure you've noticed some of the bruises she has on her arms and legs. She came to school last week with a shiner and tried to cover it up with makeup. Several boys from the class teased her about it, and I sat her inside the classroom during recess and tried to have a discussion with her."

"You have no right to talk to our daughter without our permission," the mother started in again. "In fact, maybe we should pull her out and find another school."

"I'm not your enemy, Mrs. Gibbs. I'm trying to help Cora. I'm trying to help the two of you. I think we need to pay attention to several things I've observed."

"So, a kid can't be clumsy? She runs into things," said the woman who herself had a very large bruise at her wrist as if someone had yanked on it. Martel knew it was possible the mother didn't want to come to terms with just what was happening in their home for her own set of reasons.

"There's more than just the bruising." Martel tried to make eye contact with Cora's father but was unable to. His eyes were downcast. Martel's heart sank.

Mrs. Gibbs stood, nervously. "I gotta have a cigarette. Where can I go?"

"You can go sit in your car and have one, if you like."

"Gimme the keys," she said to her husband, again without looking him in the eyes. She held her hand out, and Martel saw the obvious signs of a knife cut nearly three inches long, extending from her wrist toward her elbow joint.

When Mrs. Gibbs left, the door remained open, which was a blessing, Martel thought. She heard sounds of birds who had built nests in the upper reaches of the hallway outside. There were sounds of a lawnmower and a leaf blower, children playing outside, and cars from a nearby expressway. She focused on the world going by outside, a world she wanted to run into and enjoy.

Mr. Gibbs was silent. He crossed his legs, balanced his chin on his fingers, and continued to stare at the ground.

"Are the two of you having troubles?" she asked him. She chastised herself for posing something perhaps too personal.

He gave her a half smile. "You could say that." He shifted his legs again. "My wife's a very disturbed woman. She tries. Good hearted. But she's damaged goods." For the first time, he peered back at her. "I didn't do any of that. I keep the kids away from her family as much as possible."

"Her wrist—"

"Yes, that happened about five years ago. She spent some time in the hospital after our third was born. She even tried to give the baby away."

Martel felt the hackles at the back of her neck rise. Perspiration dripped from her armpits and soaked her silk dress. A dull ache in her belly twisted her insides.

She was flooded with visions of holding Ainsley, before she knew she was Ainsley, smelling her little pink face and fingers, heartbroken that she would probably never see her again. Her nineteen-year-old self had suffered, too, but in a much different way. It was still suffering. She'd cried herself to sleep the week before she delivered, wanting to meet her baby and not wanting to experience the separation she knew was coming, that had all been planned out. If she hadn't made those arrangements, she never would have been able to say good-bye and hand the baby over to the childless couple who took her.

The Newbergs.

She wanted to ask Mr. Gibbs the question she'd heard so often spoken when people talked about adoption. "How could you—" But she knew it was a different answer for every single person faced with the impossible choice. Polite conversations were had, even though people she talked to never knew she'd experienced it. She'd given her baby up, yet she'd found a way to live with that decision, telling herself it was for the best.

And it was. It really was.

But that was her story, just one of thousands every year.

So Martel didn't ask. Instead, she gave Mr. Gibbs the out he probably deserved. "Being a parent can be very difficult. And the two of you have so many. I know it must be a struggle, even on a good day."

"There aren't many good days anymore. Honestly, when I come home, I don't know if she'll be there. I think one day she'll just take off. No warning. Just disappear. She's not a very happy person."

"But your girls—all girls?"

"Yes, ma'am. We kept trying for a boy. I got the girls genes and no boys in me."

"Well, it takes two, you know."

"No, it's me. I can't have boys. I know I can't."

Martel was trying hard to stay positive, but her lower lip was quivering. She was about to burst into tears. She managed to get out, "Are you able to ask for help? There are agencies that do that, you know. Groups who help people who get overwhelmed with being parents. Classes you can take."

"Honey," he said, his angry grey eyes squinting at her, "I only got a fourth-grade education. My classroom days are over." He was sullen, leaning toward the doorway. "Where the hell has she gone?"

Martel could see Mrs. Gibbs talking to herself, walking across the lawn from the parking lot. "She's coming. I see her." Quickly, she drew out a pamphlet from her desk drawer and handed it to him. "This is a group from a Christian church who help with this sort of thing. No classes. Just help. And no money."

He assumed his half smile again. "I don't need any-body's goddamned money. I'm no charity case."

Martel nodded. "I can clearly see that." She let him meet her eyes. She wanted to smack him right across the mouth but worked very hard not to show it. But she did give him the stare just to make a point. "No shame in asking for help. Think of your girls."

Before he could tuck the pamphlet into his pocket, Mrs. Gibbs ripped it from his fingers. "What's this?"

"Just a suggestion for the both of you. I know rais-ing children—"

"Do you have any kids?" Mrs. Gibbs interrupted.

That was a difficult question to answer.

"No."

"Then you can take your literature and shove it." Mrs. Gibbs threw it down on the desk. Martel quietly slipped it back into the drawer from where it came.

"Are you done?" Mr. Gibbs asked her.

"No, I was just beginning. Please sit," she directed the mother.

"This is a fucking waste of time," she said.

Martel took a drink of water, sat up straight, and continued. "I found Cora today with her pants down around her ankles, standing behind the field shed. She was letting two boys touch her down there. That's not the kind of behavior a fifth grader should be exhibiting. It means she's learned it from someone else, perhaps an older child or an adult. Probably a male. If I were her parents, I'd want to find out who that male is, and I'd want to get some help for Cora, or it may progress into something else much worse." She watched the shocked expression on both their faces. She was glad this was news and not something they expected. "Because this person might be preying on others, maybe one of your other girls too. This type of behavior is learned, and it has to stop."

Mrs. Gibbs burst into tears. Martel had struck a nerve, and the woman appeared to be reliving some pain from her past. She suspected it didn't have anything to do with Cora, either. And, for the first time, she saw Mr. Gibbs show some tenderness for his wife. He placed his arm around her shoulder and wouldn't let her shrug it off, even though she tried several times. Finally, she sunk into his shoulder and sobbed.

He whispered something to her. Mrs. Gibbs shook her head violently in protest.

He caught Martel's eye as his wife calmed some. "So what's next? You call the cops? Because I have a past, when I was a dumb stupid kid," Mr. Gibbs said, settling back into his chair and crossing his arms.

"I honestly don't know how all that works, but yes, I have to inform my administrator. Then, yes, the police will be notified. And Child Protective Services will want to interview her. But I'll let them explain all that to you." She scanned between the two parents. Mrs. Gibbs was wiping her face, her eyes red and puffy. She was very fragile and barely able to breathe without strain. Martel reached across the desk, holding out her hand for the woman to take. "Can I get you something? Can I call someone? Do you want to talk to someone right now, Mrs. Gibbs?"

"No, I'm fine," she quipped. Her legs were crossed, and her foot was bouncing rapidly. "That sonofabitch." She turned to her husband. "Don't you lay a hand on him, Roger, or you'll have the lot of them after me and the girls. Don't you dare. We let the cops take care of him."

"So you know who might have done this?" Martel asked.

"I'm not admitting nothing," the mother said. "Not a word of this to the girls," she scolded her husband.

"Lorene, they probably already know. Where the fuck have you been?"

Martel realized she'd have to make a full report, and she wished she'd asked her administrator to sit in. This had been a huge mistake. But, if there was one thing she was thankful for, it was that she didn't think these two damaged parents were directly responsible for the abuse Cora suffered. But Martel guessed they were probably related to someone who was.

That was going to be very tough for all of them. But

it was something that fit an ugly pattern she'd studied.

"Listen, I have no doubt someone will be in contact with you both very soon, maybe even tonight. Whatever help they offer, please take it. At least, that's my advice, for what it's worth."

"They're gonna take the kids away," Mrs. Gibbs whispered, covering her mouth with her fingers.

"They're going to want to protect them. Who is watching them now?"

"My mom."

"You need to go home and wait for the authorities."

"I'm supposed to get back to work, but I'll pack it in today."

"Does Cora come back to school on Monday?" Mrs. Gibbs asked.

"There's no reason she can't. She hasn't been a danger to anyone but herself. However, we do have to thoroughly investigate, so let's see what happens over the weekend. I think, for her own good, I'll keep her in with me during recess if she does. I don't want any bullying or teasing going on at her expense. And of course, I won't be saying anything to the other kids, just to my administrator. I do believe the school is a safe place for your daughter. And we'll keep a special eye on her. But I don't know what the administrator will want to do."

Mrs. Gibbs nodded.

"I have your phone number, and I'll call you this weekend, if you want. And here's my cell phone. Give me a call if you need anything."

Mr. Gibbs stood and shook Martel's hand again. "Can I have that brochure back?"

"You bet. Here you go."

After they left, she watched them hug in the parking lot, get into their car, and then drive away. Martel chose to believe the young couple were of the same mind with the same purpose. But that was just a guess on her part.

She called the administrator, and after they met, he agreed to call the Pinellas County sheriff's department, as well as Social Services. He told her to fill out her incident report at home over a glass of wine and email it to him when she finished. He admonished her to get it in this evening.

"Next time, don't tackle this by yourself. One of the counselors would have sat in with you."

"Yes, I couldn't find anyone, but you're right. I worried too many strangers in the room would cause a negative reaction. But I can see that was a mistake."

"Go home, Martel. But get me that report, agreed?"

"Absolutely."

HER HANDS SHOOK on the drive back to her bungalow.

She clutched the steering wheel like it was a lifeline, digging her nails into the black leatherette covering.

She entered her living room, turned on some peaceful instrumental music, dumped her computer case and purse on the couch, kicked off her shoes, and poured herself a glass of white wine, taking one very long sip. She changed into a pair of sweats and treated her feet to her favorite pair of felt slippers.

The late afternoon sun melted low on the horizon, turning the sand and puffy clouds outside a deep rose-peach color. The bright glow reflected off her walls and warmed her face as she stood facing the sliding glass door overlooking the bay, sipping her wine. Her thoughts drifted back to the recollection she'd had of the baby in her arms all too briefly.

Now twelve years old, Ainsley was slightly older than Cora. The discovery of the abuse today had shaken her all the way to the bottoms of her feet. If she had a magic wand she could brush over the land, she'd make a perfect world for young girls like her daughter to live a normal life away from the fear of predators. She had to help nail this person or persons. It was a rescue she was embarking on, even though Cora belonged to another family. She cared enough to stay involved until the case was solved and then would need to care enough to walk away.

Like she'd done years ago.

She poured herself another glass of wine and sat at

her computer, wrote her report, and emailed it to her administrator. Before she closed her laptop, she sent Damon an email.

'Can't wait to see you tomorrow and wish I could stay longer. Looking forward to a nice walk on your beach, discovering all the way its magic heals everything just like my beach does here in Florida. Packing now, drinking wine, and missing you terribly.'

While she was loading up her suitcase, she heard the ping of her cell phone with Damon's response.

'I can't wait. But I'm warning you, I might not ever let you go.'

'Music to my ears, my love.'

'Then let's do it. Let's run away.'

Damon's answer brought hot tears that spilled over her cheeks. Her delicious longing for him was causing her pain and, at the same time, filled her with joy.

'We will, Damon. First, we'll have the vows in June, the party with all your drunk SEAL friends, and you looking handsome in your dress whites. I want the spectacle of it all—at my beach at sunset.'

'Your wish is my command. Hurry.'

It was a glorious time to be alive, to be jumping out of that airplane and going for the freefall ride of her life. An adventure unlike any other she'd ever had.

After this weekend, she knew her life would never be the same.

CHAPTER 3

MARTEL'S FLIGHT WAS due in at noon, but this morning, Damon was commanded to the Team 3 building on base for an informational meeting on their next deployment, coming up sometime within the next month.

"Surprise, surprise. We got a sex trafficking ring still operating in Baja California, guys. I know that comes as a shock to you all, but that's what we've got. So dust off your tropical pink flamingo shirts and your rubber zoris, and start practicing being a tourist," Kyle Lansdowne said to the group.

Their State Department rep took over the floor next. He already wore a green and yellow pineapple shirt, sipping water from a glass with a purple paper umbrella sticking out of the top. He spoke to the group behind a pair of sunglasses.

"Carter Ridgeway here. I'm pleased to make your acquaintance. I don't want any of you to get the wrong idea. These rings that deal in drugs and girls—children, really—are all over the world. You throw a dart at the continent of Africa, South America, Mexico, even the United States, parts of Europe, Middle East, and beyond, and you'll probably hit the location of one of these rings. As soon as we get one put to bed, another takes its place."

It wasn't anything that surprised Damon.

"We have a different wrinkle in that we have issues at the border during the past three, four years, but now it's escalated to enormous proportions. We have a lack of manpower and changes in policy regarding undocumented workers. Add in the mix, we have drug dealers and coyotes who are making a fortune while we're all trying to sort out the most humanitarian way to deal with the problem. Which is what we stand for, gents. We want it to be safe and humane but effective. Meanwhile, the other side doesn't play by the same rules. So we're stuck."

Several comments were whispered around the room. Damon saw Kelly Fielding and Sven Tolar standing at the back of the building, sharing a coffee. They toasted him, and he nodded in return, which caused others to turn their heads and notice.

Ridgeway continued. "As a bit of background, I've been wearing my Special Agent badge now for ten years, and for the last five of those, I'm been taking stealth teams to various embassies all over the world, evacuating U.S. citizens undercover from hostile places where Americans shouldn't be, in my humble opinion. So it might surprise you to know that nearly ten thousand US citizens are still trapped in a few of these places. Some were NGOs, some were doing humanitarian missions, some sent by news agencies and churches. And some, believe it or not, are tourists."

The whole room erupted in whispers and light conversation.

"Now lately, we've seen an uptick in the desire for younger American girls and boys for the sex trafficking business. Those kids get sold all over the world, and once they are, they are really hard to find. We're talking less than thirty percent, maybe even lower, are recovered. In fact, we've been prioritizing groups to rescue based on the number of children these family units have traveling or living with them, because they've become very valuable targets for these cretins who deal in the flesh trade."

A number of their last SEAL Team 3 missions had involved the sex trafficking pirates in Africa and the Canary Islands. But the Team had also been to Mexico on previous deployments before Damon joined up.

"You're gonna ask me how come all these people take their kids to these places and get caught. Some work in rural areas, villages where there isn't internet and barely cell phone service. Sometimes things can change so quickly that they actually travel by accident into the middle of a militia turf war. Or they think living with their friendlies will keep them safe, until someone's army comes through and decides to make an example of them. Two years ago, I rescued a whole family—they were ecotourists—who lived in the jungles in the Amazon for months before we could get them. These are good people, and they deserve to come home."

Kyle stepped forward and began adding to the presentation. "Special Agent Ridgeway uncovered a group in Honduras, an American soccer team down there for exhibition matches with local kids, kidnapped at gunpoint, a whole bus full of them, along with some local kids and international coaches, and successfully returned them home. At the end of that mission, he discovered parts of the ring escaped, infiltrating a huge migrant caravan, where there would be less scrutiny, and they were cherry-picking girls from that group, separating them from their parents and removing them quietly under everyone's noses.

"Ridgeway tracked them to Baja, where they've set up a complex of abandoned hotels and basic prisons to house their booty. He then requested help from our community. So our mission is to draw out as many of the leaders as possible and bring them to a black ops site State maintains near San Felipe at an abandoned Mexican air base perfect for extraction. From there, we'll be going down the finger toward Cabo to disrupt as much of their operation we can get our hands on. But it's only a matter of time before we'll run into Mexican Government resistance or from a faction in the government making money off the enterprise. We have some good partners we're working with in Mexico. It's much better in some ways and much worse because of the sheer numbers. But it only takes a few bad actors, and the missions get real complicated real quick."

Ridgeway continued. "You fellas have posed as fishing enthusiasts before, and that worked well. We asked for your Team because of your experience and familiarity with how these groups work. You successfully shut down the Cortez brothers' network. And this one and several others have replaced it, capitalizing from the vacuum created when you took the brothers out."

Damon saw lots of heads nodding. He could feel the Team getting pumped up with that old "force for good" pride he often felt himself.

"So here's one thing we have to be careful of. Their tactics have changed. If the cartel gets close to being captured, they murder all the victims and just disappear into the countryside, waiting to come back and strike once again with new prey later on, rather than stay and fight over the girls. The danger level has amped up significantly. We're losing a lot of Border Patrol agents, but now more than ever, children are being used and often discarded later, sort of like a disposable entry ticket into the US. Younger kids are used because they're easy to steal, easy to transport because they're small, generally more compliant than older children, and very easy to kill, unfortunately."

The room erupted in groans and curses.

Kyle completed the short meeting after some logistics were discussed. He introduced Sven Tolar and Kelly Fielding to the group of newbies. The legendary FSB warrior from Norway and the State Department liaison held hands and waved to the crowd.

"Damon, you be careful. I think these two want to come to your wedding, and they might piggyback on all Martel's hard planning. Watch 'em. If you're not careful, it will be a foursome."

The people in the room laughed.

It was going to be a warm day as he made it out to his Hummer. He'd worn a white long-sleeved shirt and his jeans. He took Coop's direction and had gotten a quick haircut last night, taking extra care to give himself a close shave this morning. He was headed to the airport.

He heard whistling behind him.

Fredo, T.J., and Tucker were clustered together, catcalling him.

"Lookin' very snappy there, son!" barked Tucker.

"Very tight and spiffy, tadpole," added T.J.

"Oh, you gonna get laid tonight for sure," Fredo finished.

This wasn't helping his case of nerves one bit. He turned without commenting, but they wouldn't stop. Finally, T.J. caught up to him.

"Bring her to the beach tonight. We've got a little pre-Valentine bonfire going on, in case you didn't hear."

"I'm sure I'll have other plans," Damon tossed back at the three. "You guys just want to look at her. I know you too well."

"We live for you single guys. Come on, give us a break," said Tucker.

"I'll ask her. You know she's only staying tonight. Tomorrow, she's leaving."

"Oh, I get it, she doesn't think you can last longer than one long night? Or is that all she can stand?" teased T.J.

The other two howled at the comment.

"You guys are assholes. She's gotta go up to the Bay Area to visit friends tomorrow. And she has to be at work on Monday. She'll be back." Damon hadn't told many about his past or about Ainsley. He definitely wasn't going to bring it up now.

"Or you might ditch the mission." Fredo winked, adding a nod for good measure.

"What did you get her? I wanna see," T.J. whispered.

Damon stood tall, pressed his chest out, and grinned. "You're lookin' at it."

"Oh, wow. Damon, my man, you gotta very long, painful evening coming up," said Fredo. "That's just not smart. You gotta work harder than that."

"I can work very hard," he smiled, raising his eyebrows.

"Not sure she'll see it that way," T.J. scowled.

He was now starting to get pissed off, so he stopped, put his hands on his hips, and lectured all three of them. He needed to put an end to their teasing.

"Look, it goes like this. Flowers? She's traveling tomorrow, first to San Francisco and then back on the plane to Tampa on the red eye. I don't think she wants to toss a sixty-dollar bouquet of roses in the trash, right?"

They nodded.

"Fancy lingerie? I don't think we have time to properly enjoy that. I'll wait until we have a whole week to ourselves to introduce some of that. Suggestions welcomed. And I'm taking up an offering, in case you are so inclined."

All three of his buds had their arms crossed, now avidly listening… or pretending to.

"And what's the point of getting a fancy hotel room? The Hotel Del is booked. So is the dining room, and I'm hoping we'll be focusing on other things, not the quality of the drapes or the view. She wants to walk the beach and feel the sunset. I plan to give her both those things, and more." He finished it off with a smile then added, "So fuck off!"

HE WAS MORE anxious than he wanted to be, sort of like the first time he deployed, which was silly because they'd spent lots of time together since they reconnected. He couldn't shake loose the jitters, regardless. It was so important that everything be perfect. That's why he didn't want to plan anything. He was going to let her make all the decisions, since her big day was coming up tomorrow, when she got to meet Ainsley for the first time. God, how he wished he could be there with her.

So maybe Martel would be nervous, a little extra sensitive. That was to be expected, he thought. No biggie. Maybe she'd cry a little more when she talked about things or might take stuff in a strange way. Women were complicated, especially thoughtful women like Martel. Women who cared about people and weren't out there to just party. He didn't want to disappoint her. A nice, quiet evening with a good bottle of her favorite wine was all that was necessary. There would be time enough later on to get acquainted with the other guys, some of whom might come across rude or insensitive…

Oh fuck. I'm doomed!

No amount of self-talk was working today. He was going to sweat through this shirt, would be hugging her at the airport with huge basketball-sized sweat circles beneath his armpits. He could smell his aftershave burning off already, and the scent to follow wouldn't be nearly as pleasant. And he hadn't brought a fresh shirt. He should have thought about another tee shirt too. And now his pants felt a size too small. Had he gained weight? Would she think he looked flabby? He hadn't had time to get a proper tan, but the haircut she'd probably appreciate. Suddenly, he remembered she'd told him one time she liked his hair on the longer side.

Which way is it? he wondered as he entered the airport short term parking garage. He was a bit early, so perhaps he'd have a beer, and that might help—or a shot of Jack, maybe—but then he'd smell of alcohol, and she wouldn't like that either. Breathing into his palm, he wondered if his breath was bad but couldn't tell because his hand still smelled of aftershave.

He tweeted his Hummer locked and jogged across

the concrete into the airport building itself. It was crowded and loud. He bumped into a young girl who dropped her teddy bear, which was quickly run over by a rolling suit carrier gripped in the hand of a man wearing a long green camo rain slicker. The man nearly tripped over his own feet as the suitcase stopped while his legs continued. He flipped his left arm out to the side to balance himself and slapped a paper coffee cup right out of a young woman's hand, which spilled down the front of her blouse and onto the gentleman in a suit walking beside her.

The woman, startled, dropped her cell phone on the travertine floor and watched it scoot nearly ten feet, hit the side of the lobby wall like a hockey puck, and took a ricochet shot right into the path of a ten-passenger electric transport vehicle barreling down the hallway to make a late gate assignment. The driver in a red vest tried to swerve to avoid running over the cell phone but clipped a handcart burdened with three precariously perched and overstuffed plastic garbage cans. One tipped off, spilling contents onto the pathway of a group of women Lacrosse players.

As papers and food wrappers spread out over the floor, someone's emotional support dog got loose and ran with its leash trailing to intercept a dirty diaper opened wide and fully exposed, resembling a melted chocolate croissant. The dog's owner pulled at the little mutt as he attempted to get away, dodging around and between oncoming pedestrian traffic. A toddler stepped right across the paper mess, including making a four-inch shoe-sized impression in the brown diaper detritus and then attempted to walk farther with it stuck to the bottom of his foot for several steps until he tripped and sat right in the smelly substance.

The toddler earned a nasty look from his mother, who changed course with the little one in tow, the deflection causing her to bump into a luggage cart which toppled a dozen suitcases piled precariously high by an inexperienced young valet. One of the suitcases burst open, and several people nearly tripped over it, but one heavyset man carrying a guitar case stepped accidentally on a corner, which caused the case to flip into the air and then land a few feet away.

By this time, Damon had caught up to the case, having negotiated through the string of messes behind him that made the wide approach to the arrival lobby look more like there was some kind of protest going on. He didn't stop to right the case but quickly made his way up to the arrival lounge where there was a bar. He definitely was going to have that drink now, after he'd nearly talked himself out of it earlier.

Damon slipped in between two people with their backs turned to each other, one a woman and one a man, and ordered a neat shot. As he brought the glass to his lips, he heard a familiar, "Oh. My God. It's Damon!" from the woman on his right, which caused just enough of a jerk to his arm that he spilled some of the drink on the front of his white and very unforgiving shirt.

Dammit. Dammit. Dammit.

He slurped the rest of it quickly, smacked the glass back on the bar, and chanced a look.

It was as bad as he thought it was. Charlene, his ex, extended her rather large boobs in his direction, and he tried hard not to look, but it was no use. She was poured into her black very tight and very shiny skinny pants and wore ginormous four-inch heels and one of those fuzzy low-cut white sweaters that used to make him sneeze. He'd developed an allergy for sure to the Angora or arctic squirrel or whatever it was that those things were made out of.

Get. A. Grip.

"Well, if it isn't the old flame that still burns. And it's Valentine's Day. How perfect," she purred, batting her enhanced eyelashes with the red accents applied. "You know, I woke up this morning, and I was dreaming about you and that body of yours, Damon. We made a pretty good pair, don't you think?"

"Charlene. What a surprise." His stomach was flopping around like a near-dead fish.

"I'm off to Vegas. Wanna come?" she cooed. Her

lips came dangerously close to his.

He backed up and stepped on the gentleman's shoe behind him. He had to get out of there.

"Those days are gone, I'm afraid. I'm here to pick up my—my *fiancée!*"

"Oh, how wonderful. I'd like to meet her."

"Not going to happen." He placed a five-dollar bill on the counter, checked the time, and noted it was still early, but he probably had enough time to wash the little light brown stain off the front of the shirt and, if he was lucky, dry it with the electric hand dryer. "I gotta run, but it was nice seeing you."

He heard the clickity clack of her heels behind him as she worked her little buns off to keep up with his long strides. This wasn't happening, he told himself. Now he was being chased by his ex, and he had alcohol on his breath and a stain on his once perfect shirt.

"Wait! Wait, Damon. I just wanted to tell you something."

He didn't pay attention. The loudspeaker was saying something about an arriving flight and the noise behind him blocked most of it out. He glanced at the monitor next to him until he found the flight information for Tampa.

Arrived early!

Due to the brief stop to check, Charlene had caught up to him. She placed her arms around his neck and pulled him into her chest and wouldn't let go.

"Charlene, please don't do that—" he'd started to say, but she interrupted him.

"Are you still a Navy SEAL, Damon? Because I have some great news. Jenna—"

He was searching the crowd. Several men were secretly smiling as he disentangled himself from her embrace, nearly peeling her arm from his neck as she tried one last time to grab his collar and practically ripped it.

"Stop—stop it, please, Charlene," he said, gripping her forearms and holding her firmly arm's length in front of him.

"Jenna is marrying a Navy SEAL, Damon. Isn't that great?"

He was having a hard time focusing. Did he see Martel's face in the crowd as he whirled around looking for the gate? He hoped not. Absentmindedly, he asked, "Jenna? Who—"

"My little sister. His name is Brian, and he's from Oregon. Big tall guy. A real stud, just like you," she giggled, trying to wrap her fingers around his forearms.

From behind him, he heard her voice.

"Damon?"

He quickly threw down Charlene's hands and did a one-eighty, coming face to face with Martel. Her forehead and brow wrinkled. Her mouth turned down into a frown as she leaned to the side to catch a glimpse of the blonde woman in the very tight black pants molesting him from behind.

Charlene didn't miss a beat. With one arm around his waist, the other shot out towards Martel, her red hearts charm bracelet shaking as she said, "I'm Charlene, Damon's ex. Nice to meet you, sweetie!" Charlene was hiding behind his torso, her chin resting on Damon's shoulder.

The look on Martel's face wasn't what he'd expected nor was it anything he wanted to see this Valentine's day. Her eyes focused on the stain on his shirt and followed down the length of his body and then back up again without lingering on anything in particular.

"You must be the welcoming committee. I'm Martel. I'm a *friend* of Damon's."

CHAPTER 4

MARTEL WAITED FOR Damon to clean up the mess he'd made of their meeting at the San Diego International Airport. She didn't return Charlene's happy banter and tried to ignore her altogether. She couldn't wait for the explanation he was going to stumble over, so she kept her emotions hidden and let her lack of reaction calm the waters. Charlene giggled, babbled along, and let her hands fly through the air like they were tambourines, the red hearts on her bracelet making little clicking noises.

She wondered what Damon ever saw in Charlene, which was a relief, because her former self might have gotten jealous. Today, she was just amused.

Oh, the choices we make!

She reminded herself not to be so hard on the early twenty-something Martel. She'd made some pretty poor choices too, after all. But the toughest choice of all was one of her best decisions.

Just from watching the three or four minutes between the two of them convinced her they were about as mismatched as two people could ever be. Damon was so nervous, or perhaps self-conscious, he didn't make eye contact. The two former partners would lightly toss word salads at each other until they'd just run out of things to say.

Martel was going to let them do just that.

Normally able to sleep on the plane, today's flight earlier was noisy, and her mind had been racing with the twenty or so to-do lists floating around inside her head. Some were about the wedding. Some were things she hoped she remembered to pack. Some had to do with Cora and her interchange the day before with Cora's parents. She wanted to be alone with Damon, not stuck in this airport with a thousand people crowding through it.

Charlene's nervous laughter wasn't all random. The woman snuck side glances at her to check her out.

As if she wouldn't notice.

Now Damon's ex was also talking about a mutual friend who was marrying a Navy SEAL. It was a warning beacon sent out to telegraph that Charlene was still loosely connected to the Brotherhood and probably wasn't going to leave Damon alone. This was one factor Martel hadn't counted on, but when she examined her insides, it was a minor annoyance and didn't really bother her.

Finally, Charlene's last good-bye and wink was laced with something a little dark. The woman's wounded pride was being a bully, trying to exaggerate that she was over Damon when clearly the opposite was true. Martel felt sorry for her but knew the gesture was really a veiled warning.

As Charlene's ass bounced down toward her gate, her destiny being Las Vegas, Damon put his arms around Martel's waist and turned her to face him. His sexy eyes were entirely hers to command.

"Now. Sweetheart. Love of my life. Martel." He turned her head with his thumb and forefinger at her chin. "Come here and let me show you how happy I am to have you here." His warm smile did start the process of making her panties wet. It didn't take much to just throw herself at him and plant a wet kiss on his soft lips.

"Thought you'd never ask."

"I need to get you home."

"Yes. You. Do." They walked arm in arm, heading to the luggage carousel. She let out a big sigh, glad to finally be in San Diego and clear of the talking parrot his ex reminded her of.

"Tough week?" he asked.

"Yes, you could say that." She stopped. "Damon, what was that all about?"

"What?"

"That woman. How did you—?"

"Don't ask. I'm still trying to figure out why. Sometimes you just do dumb stuff. You forgive me?"

"Nothing to forgive." She shook her head, began to laugh, and then rolled her shoulders. "You think you know someone, and they surprise you—"

"Come on, give me a break. I got those papers overseas, and you know what? I felt *liberated.* The guys were coming up and giving me the old heart-to-heart thing, and I was happy as sh—" He checked his feet. "I'm sorry about that."

"Unbelievable. Do you know how many hours I worried about your ex coming back into your life when we had to live separately for these months? I didn't expect this. I guess I feel liberated too." She gave him a quick smile and continued down the rampway.

"So you were saying there was a problem with your job at school?"

"Yes and no. I've got a problem with one of my students. I don't want to talk about it here, but we just had to refer one of my girls to Child Support Services and the police. It's just the beginning of what could be a very long and involved process."

"Oh wow. Sexual assault?" he whispered.

"Yup. Just a hunch, of course, and the first meeting I had with the parents revealed a lot. But I've just received minimal training. I'll leave it up to the experts. I sure hope we can resolve it quickly, but something tells me this is just the tip of the iceberg."

"That's too bad, especially for your last months of school there. Sounds like you don't suspect the father, or am I reading too much into this?"

"No, you're spot on, but again, it's just a hunch. They have all girls—six girls in the family. My guess is that it's someone, maybe more than one, from the wife's family." She looked up at him, his face in a deep, pensive frown. His concern made her love him even more. "But I'm not supposed to talk about it, so don't let me, okay?"

He adjusted his arm to grab her around the waist and squeezed her beside him as they continued walking toward the luggage area. "God, I missed you. It felt like half a year, and it was only, what, just shy of a month?"

"Twenty-five days. I crossed all of them off my calendar."

"How are the wedding plans coming? Or have you not had time?"

"I hired the caterer, but I'm getting the wedding cake from somewhere else. How many of your guy friends will be coming, do you know?"

"I haven't passed out any invites yet. A couple of the wives took pity on me when I talked about it. They made some 'save the date' post cards."

Martel giggled. "You're kidding, right?"

Damon shrugged. "Look, I don't do this DIY stuff. The married ladies love messing with us single guys, even the *engaged* single guys. I was going to do it today at the team meeting, but it ran over, and I had to get here."

"And you forgot to bring them. Fess up."

"Okay, yes, I forgot." His face had turned bright pink, having been caught in a white lie.

"So you know where your next mission is going to be?"

"Mexico. Baja, actually. We're looking for one particular bandido and his crew who have blended in and out of the migrant caravans, making tons of money along the way by convincing parents to give their daughters up for a better life in the U.S. Or telling them getting their daughters across the border will enhance their own chances for a successful crossing. It's so depressing to see this."

She stiffened.

Damon abruptly stopped, placed his palms under her jaw on each side. He kissed her tenderly, and whispered, "That didn't come out the way I wanted it to. We have some people actually *selling* their kids into sex rings too. Using them as an admission ticket. The coyotes work in packs, in tandem with other couples pretending to be parents who have let their daughters go with the handler, trying to convince the naïve parents they'll be safe. The whole thing is a very sorry situation. Breaks my heart, really."

She put the side of her face against his chest and listened to his beating heart, enjoying the warmth of his arms wrapped around her. Her familiar arousal was a welcome distraction to the harsh realities of the world in which they lived. "Thank you for doing what you can," she said into his chest.

He answered by kissing the top of her head.

DAMON ROLLED HER suitcase behind him as they strolled to the parking garage together.

"So did you know Charlene would be there? How did all that happen?"

"Just my unluck charm, I guess. She's between boy-friends again."

"Again? So you keep in touch?"

"Not really. I bump into her from time to time, that's all. She tries to hang around the Team 5 guys now."

"Oh yes, those rules again." Martel still didn't understand why an ex would be considered "off limits" but not a widow.

"It's a tight community. Even being careful, there's gossip, and there are some things a man and woman share when their marriage doesn't work out that has to stay private. Dirty laundry and all that. Those weren't my finest days. I don't need to be reminded of them."

She had nothing to add and didn't want to pry.

"I see on my phone the Gulf has been warm," he said as they entered the garage.

"I used to think San Diego was just as warm, but no way."

"We have a nice, clear weekend coming up. They're having another bonfire tonight, if you're interested. You can continue to get acquainted with some of the other wives."

"You steer me clear of anyone like Charlene, okay?"

"It's a deal." He unclipped the seatbelt from the side and placed it across her lap but lingered for a soft kiss. "Happy Valentine's Day, sweetheart. Just want you to know if you just want to stay in bed all afternoon and evening, I'm cool with that, too."

She watched him walk around the front of the Hummer and climb up into the driver's seat next to her. He was the sexiest man she'd ever met. Long after they'd lost touch after high school, she still dreamed about him. And just as those dreams started to fade away, they met at their mutual friends' wedding. What were the odds?

She felt silly spending so much time worrying about the chemistry between the two of them since they had to live apart. Their relationship was about as natural as it could be. This time it even felt more solid.

Damon was easy to love, and every minute she spent with him heightened her resolve to make things perfect. The problems always seemed to happen when she was all alone. The big man upstairs was telling her something alright.

She was *made* for Damon.

THE AFTERNOON SLEEPILY wound down. She had no appetite for strolling Coronado or spending hours at a seafood bar or restaurant with a view of the ocean. Her mind and desires were here and now, in his arms, in his bed, re-exploring all the reasons she was going to uproot herself and become a San Diego transplant.

Their prolonged lovemaking turned her bones to rubber. She could easily forget all her stress and worry, the apprehension of giving up a place she loved so strongly. It gave her focus. Each scorching hot kiss continued to obliterate her doubts. He was patient and relentless, taking her powerfully and not stopping until she'd reached the pinnacle of her passion first. She loved his control, the way his body and soul consumed hers. Left panting and without an ounce of resistance, the only thing she could do was surrender to him completely and try to match his ardor with the strength of her own.

It would be impossible to forget him again, and she hoped she would never have to try.

THEY ARRIVED AT the Team bonfire on the beach when the sky had turned deep navy blue and the stars were out. Jameson Daniels, one of Damon's brothers who used to be a fairly famous country star in Nashville, brought out his guitar, and his seven-year-old daughter, Charlotte, brought out hers, which was the size of a ukulele. The two of them sang for the group. Charlotte had a very strong and sweet voice.

After a handful of ballads, Charlotte was pulled away by some of the other SEAL children, so Jameson played a few songs he'd been working on.

"He's really good. I think I remember him," Martel said.

"You've met him before."

"Yes, but I mean, before—well, years ago. Something familiar about him."

Damon stared into her eyes with no expression.

"What?" she asked him.

"So maybe you were one of his groupies. He said he had a girl in every city. I'll bet you were Santa Rosa."

"I don't think so. Not sure we were big enough for the likes of him. You remember what it was like. Everyone was more into classic VWs and fast sports cars. Pickup trucks weren't considered cool. I don't ever remember listening to country growing up. You were into classic rock."

"Got that from my folks."

She watched Daniels tip his hat and quietly put away his guitar. His wife, Lizzy, now extremely big with another girl, they'd been told, gave him a big hug and kiss. Martel was touched nearly to the point of tears, watching their family unit. It was her vow that this time, the second time around, she would have what they had.

Damon introduced her again to several others on the team. She was disappointed Christy Lansdowne wasn't there. Kyle was trying to babysit his three and zoomed past them several times, frantically running back and forth in search of one or another of them.

Martel easily made the connection she'd hoped she would. This was now going to be her life. These were going to be the people she would depend on, learn about, and support.

She had expected to turn in early, but they took a moonlit stroll down the beach and then made love in the dunes.

"I hoped you wouldn't be disappointed I didn't buy you anything, Martel. I just wanted to be with you."

"It was the perfect Valentine's Day—one I'll remember forever. If this little trip was any longer, you probably wouldn't be able to get me to leave."

"And that," he said as he kissed her, "was exactly what I was going for."

On the way back to his rental, he added, "Make sure you tell Ainsley that I love her, okay? We created a little miracle, you and I."

"And we're just getting started," Martel whispered back. "I'll make sure she knows she's loved. That's the whole purpose of the meeting. We gave her the best start we could have. But I want her to know we did it out of love."

CHAPTER 5

I T WAS HARDER than Damon had thought saying good-bye the next day. Martel's plane ride was going to be a quick hour-long hop from San Diego to San Jose, where she would pick up a car and get checked into her hotel. And then she'd have that meeting with their daughter.

"You know I don't really want to go alone, Damon," Martel whispered as they drove to the airport.

"I do. But we're playing by the rules. Playing nice and careful. I get it. There's more to it than what either of us wants. We have her family to consider. I hope she lets me come next time."

"Same here. Maybe we rushed this too much. Seems like I'm making sausage here. Squeezing in a trip to see you, quick trip to see her, and then, wham, back at school with all the other stuff going on there. I should have taken a week off."

"But you got the invite, and they were specific on

the date. So we had to do it this way. Besides, you won't be with your classroom next year, so you've got a lot of things to finish up. And you're planning a wedding. Just face it, sweetheart, you're going to be overmaxed for a few months. We'll relax on the honeymoon. I have one deployment coming up and maybe another one. These days, anything could happen. I could be back in Africa or South America next time. Who knows?"

"True. I just don't like to do anything this important so rushed," she gently suggested.

He felt her misgivings. He knew it was taxing her, having so many details hanging out in the breeze. She'd want to nail down every one.

"You could have just eliminated the trip to see me. But I'm glad you didn't." He watched her blush and shy smile, something he'd always love.

"I *had* to do that." And then, "But you're right, Damon. I've just got to embrace the rush. Keep my head on straight."

Damon knew she was nervous but would never admit it. That probably weighed on her as well. Ever the over-achiever, Martel had lists for everything and loved checking things off. She used big sticky notes on her wall for making project lists, like she was running a whole SEAL Team. It was kind of amusing to watch. But that's what made her such a good teacher, he noted.

As they pulled into the short-term parking area, he stopped the car and turned to her. People passed the car, traveling back and forth, bearing luggage and armfuls of carryon bags while the two of them sat in silence. "Martel, you're going to do just fine. Don't worry about anything. No way to know how it's going to turn out, so just be okay with however it does. Don't beat yourself up if it goes—differently."

He didn't want to put a negative connotation on it but needed to bring it up.

"But call me, okay? I don't want you stewing about something."

She gave him a timid smile. "Thanks. I do like planning everything out, don't I?"

He rolled his eyes and fanned his face with his fingers. "You think? Just know you can't control everything. On the teams, we plan for anything and everything and still it never goes the way we intend it. Never. There's nothing you can do but just enjoy meeting her and doing what you came to do: telling her that she is loved. *By both of us.* Hopefully making it so we can see her again, maybe together. That's all you can do."

"You're right. And we have a lot to be grateful for. The Newbergs have been wonderful. I want them to know that, too. It's such a gift they're even allowing me to see her."

"You did that. You chose nice people, Martel. Give yourself credit. Now they're treating you with the same respect you gave them."

"I want to do it right."

"You'll do it your way, Martel. I have no doubt it will be right. Come on, let's get you on the plane."

He wheeled her bag to the ticket counter, stood with her while she got her boarding pass, and checked her bag. Just outside the TSA checkpoint, they sat for a glass of wine and a beer, holding hands. He watched as several young men, looking like new Navy recruits, passed by wearing backpacks, acting like he did when he first reported to base after the training in Great Lakes. They behaved like kids on a football team. Excited, hiding their fears, trying to be a good friend to the guy on their right or left who was going through all the same jumble of emotions. Everyone wanted to be one of the ones who made it, not to have to report home and say they DORed—dropped on request. And yet, the odds were stacked against them. Always.

It would always be the same, class after class. Wave after wave of strong young men pushing their limits.

He knew what he was going to do later on this afternoon after her plane took off.

"I'll take pictures for you," she mumbled, ringing the top of her wine glass with her finger.

"Did you bring pictures of us?"

"I did. Got a nice one of us at Sunset Beach with the salmon-colored sky in the background, too." She smiled, removing her finger from the glass and folding her hands in her lap. "I brought pictures of my mom and dad, the house I grew up in. My dog. A picture of you from the yearbook I loved, the one in your basketball uniform. I'm standing next to you."

"I remember that picture. We'd just won the championship."

"You were the star. Always have been." Her eyes were warm and filled with tears.

He took her hand in both of his. "Hey, what's making you sad?"

"I'm worried about her questions."

"Well, just be honest with her. That's what we agreed, right?"

"What if I don't have an answer for a question she asks? You know, what if she asks me one of those tough ones?"

He put his arm around her shoulders and pulled her close. "They're all going to be tough questions. If they weren't, she wouldn't want to know anything about you. About us. And you'll have to make that okay, if that happens, Martel. Be prepared that she won't be that interested or scared to ask you anything. She's only twelve. Shoot, I was afraid of my own shadow at twelve."

Martel lay her head against him and thought about that for a bit. Then she slowly wound out of his arms and stood up, putting her computer bag strap over her shoulder. "I think it's time."

The long hug and even longer kiss didn't calm her nerves. He felt her heart beating like it was going to run down the hallway and out into oncoming traffic. Her hands were shaking and a little cold. Her smile was chaste and not full. He loved her so much and more every day. What could he do to help her?

Only one thing he could do.

"Martel, I just want to say how damn lucky I am that you came back into my life after those years when I was such an idiot. Just remember, you bring love to everything you do, honey. You make the world a better place just because you're in it. Go bring her some of that sunshine. She'll love meeting you. I hope she understands how lucky she is to have a person like you. Not everyone gets to have someone who loves them like you do. You can tell her from me, she and I, we are the lucky ones."

Her eyes were weeping, but she smiled through her tears.

"Thank you, Damon. It's all happening now. This is the big stuff, isn't it? I've thought about this day ever since her birth. I love you so much—" She grabbed him one last time then turn and walked into the TSA line without looking back.

He stood there, watching until she made her way to the rampway leading to the gates. At last, she turned and waved with a brave smile, holding her ticket over her head.

As she disappeared into the crowd, he felt like a piece of him had been torn out of his chest.

Damon drove to the Hotel Del Coronado and parked in an unmetered spot. He walked through the lush grounds, winding through an open-air restaurant and two-story bar area overlooking the ocean. He walked in front of it until he got onto the beach and then headed south.

When he was going through BUD/S, they had done their rubber boat exercises there on the beach, carrying them over their heads in crews of eight or ten or twelve. Sometimes the short ones, sometimes the tall ones, sometimes the mixed-up ones which were hardest on the tall guys like Damon.

He still had a patch at the back of his head where he could swear the hair had been rubbed off and would never really re-grow. But maybe it was his imagination.

He remembered some of the faces of the guys who lay beside him, shivering in the cold early morning surf, the wet-n-sandys. It reminded him of the times when he'd look up at the stars and the moon and feel that cold pang of ocean creeping up onto his almost warmed but very wet uniform, boots and all, making him an icebox again, until the water would recede and his body's heater began to work overtime again to warm the water close to his skin. Then the surf claimed him again.

Over and over, it went. He never thought about how it stunk to be doing this. He just did it. In making it not significant, he could endure a lot more. It was always harder whenever he worried about surviving a phase.

He remembered how green his feet had been when he finally got to take his boots off after six days without showering, warmth, or sleep.

He remembered the line of blue, green, and red helmets, each with a name hand-painted by the recruit. These were the DOR guys, a reminder that some had chosen to go home or had decided the process wasn't worth the pain they were suffering. Sometimes, the guys just discovered their level of want or how far they had to test themselves. Some of these fellows he didn't know very well. Others, he did. Some were roommates or swim buddies. Then, one day, they were just gone. Nobody lingered around. They were either in or out. Some were made to chase the bell on the back of the pickup truck barreling down the beach, the instructors in their warm jackets yelling catcalls at them to ring the bell. He never got to the point where he'd suffer that humiliation.

Except it wasn't. To even try out for the teams was being a hero. So many hurdles had to be overcome just to get the chance. Part of it was luck, but most of it was not quitting. He wasn't very good at much, but he was good at not quitting, and so he became a recruit and eventually wore the Trident proudly.

He could still hear the shouts the instructors barked, the answering, shivering, miserable hoarse callbacks, and the grunts when someone fell or threw up or fell out of a boat and had to be hauled inside. He'd been on the last boat crew, relegated to an extra thirty-minute swim in the dirty inlet. Sometimes, he'd made the fastest boat crew. He'd been on the crew with foreign trainees who didn't try half as hard as the rest of them had to. He'd had to pick up some of the slack for some who were lazy, sick, or disheartened. It wasn't being soft. It was about being a team.

There was no other training in life like this training. And it didn't even begin to train him how to be a good person, husband, or father. While he was out there doing all that, he had been oblivious to what Martel was going through. Their baby was growing, and she was preparing to place her up for adoption. Martel was handling all the burdens, alone, no team to back her up. Just her mother, the nurses at the home she stayed at, and the grit that was Martel.

Because she wasn't a quitter either. And, like she said, she thought about meeting Ainsley every day since she gave birth to her. This was the day she'd finally do it. Cross that thing off her list. Stare into the eyes and face of the little girl she carried, they made together, the little girl who deserved to know she came from them, even though they were not her parents. Someone else stepped up to the plate and got to claim that one.

He and Martel just hadn't quit on her.

They didn't quit on the love that they'd once had and now had again. Even with the burden of the mistakes. It wasn't always going to be easy. They would never be perfect. But he knew, he was certain, they would never quit.

No matter what.

CHAPTER 6

T HE TREE-LINED STREETS of old Palo Alto reminded Martel of the McDonald neighborhood in Santa Rosa where she'd lived during part of her childhood. Although the houses were much larger here on the peninsula, especially recently with the McMansions mushrooming from small bungalows in the trendy neighborhoods, the feel was the same. With the wider streets and old oaks, lush formal gardens lovingly tended, it was perhaps California's answer to Savannah, on a much smaller scale.

She'd ridden her bicycle to her music lessons and dance classes and been on teen boards at the Santa Rosa Youth Center, where the real action was. The dance parties and plays were her favorite, since she didn't do much with sports.

Later on, as her interest in boys developed, she watched basketball and football, even some soccer. The teen dances had become a problem with a downtown that was in search of itself and city leaders who didn't have the will to imprint a clear vision for the youth. She wondered if Palo Alto suffered the same fate.

The Newbergs lived in a brown shingled, mock Tudor style home on a quiet cul-de-sac street. At the end of the street, a quaint park/sitting area had been created, dotted with more than a dozen multicolored birdhouses mounted on poles. It appeared to be a neighborhood project, and the place was literally covered in little birds, mostly finches, landing and taking off, scaring off other birds and showing off their plumery. People had fashioned houses out of old boots, buckets and paint cans, galvanized watering cans, and old telephone boxes. One was even made out of a small pink Barbie house with glittering ribbons hanging down, blowing in the gentle late afternoon breeze.

She parked in a cut-out area of the lawn and walked toward the Newberg's simple but neatly mani-cured home. She heard a dog bark nearby when she rang the doorbell.

Ainsley answered the door, looking even more like Damon, her father, than the picture the Newbergs had given her a month ago. She was very tall for her age, her eyes a bright ocean blue, with a cute, upturned nose and a saddle of light brown freckles pouring all over her rosy cheeks. Her spun-gold blonde hair was tied in braids but mussed. Dressed in a basketball uniform, Martel guessed she'd either just come from practice or had been practicing in the front yard. She hadn't missed the basketball hoop attached to the double-car garage door frame.

She'd grown up fast, Martel guessed, because she wasn't entirely confident in her size, nearly Martel's height. Her feet were enormous. She sported athletic shoes with multicolored laces. Drawings of daisies and hearts adorned the sides in bright permanent markers.

"I don't wear them for games. For practice," she said, responding to the fact that Martel had been apparently gawking at them. Her voice was slightly raspy and uneven.

"Ainsley, they're beautiful. I was just admiring the patterns. You like to draw, I take it?"

"Not really," the teen shrugged. "I just didn't want them to look like basketball shoes."

A perfect explanation.

Not sure whether or not she should shake her hand, Martel introduced herself. "I'm so happy you agreed to meet with me."

Ainsley shrugged again. "Sure. Why not? You gotta right."

And there it was, that little prick of a pin that burst her warm, friendly bubble. The air seeped out of the thought she could control this little drama play between them. It was Ainsley's show, and Martel was just here for the ride she'd allow her to take. Come what may. Damon had warned her about that.

Mark and Lori Newberg were standing behind Ainsley and invited her inside.

"Oh, sorry. Duh!" Ainsley said, standing aside to make room for her entry, making a face at her father, who mimicked her right back. Lori smiled and kept her eyes on Martel.

"Thank you, Lori and Mark. I really appreciate you setting this up."

"Of course," Lori said, with respect.

Martel felt a bond and trust between the two of them immediately. It didn't ease her nerves, however.

"Come on, Beans, let's get this group some re-freshments," Mark said to Ainsley. "You want wine, beer, water, or soda?" He pointed in Martel's direction.

"I'll just have water."

"Fart or no-fart," asked Ainsley, her hands on her hips, one knee bent. She more resembled a young colt than a girl.

"I'm sorry?" Martel was confused.

"She means gas or no gas. Her spin on the little choice there," added Mark.

Martel laughed. "I see. Quite unusual. I can see she's her own person."

While everyone stared at Ainsley, the girl pulled her shirt from her chest, examined herself, and said,

"Nope. No one else in there. I'm the only person in this body—today, anyway."

"I'll take the farted water, please, then." Martel answered.

"Make that two, Mark," yelled Lori.

"Coming right up!"

Lori motioned to a loveseat across from a leather-covered reading chair and matching leather couch at forty-five-degree angles. Martel sat in the loveseat and waited. Lori chose the large reading chair, crossed her legs, and leaned over her thigh.

"You can see we have our hands full. Ainsley is the center of our attention, the life of this family. It's never a dull moment." She tried to look overworked, but Martel knew otherwise.

"She's very bright. Quite a character."

"She and Mark play a lot of basketball together. He played in college some and helps out with the team. When she wanted to take ballet, he learned ballet himself so he could practice with her, help her with her lifts and stretches. That didn't last long, and I'm glad too. The sight of my husband in tights—well, he has skinny legs."

They both laughed.

"Sounds like they have a perfect relationship, Lori. I'm so pleased to see how happy she is."

"We're very proud of her. It's almost like she was

meant for us. Having her in our lives is so perfect. I've thought about it many times, how similar she and Mark are in so many ways. People assume she's biological, not that it matters."

There was a little lump in Martel's throat forming. That pain in her gut that Damon had missed out on something wonderful. She drew in the thought she came up with many times like this when she was filled with regret: She'd done the right thing, and she hadn't been in any position to raise her daughter. These people were. And that was as it should be.

She inhaled and asked a question she'd always wanted to know. "What did she say when you told her about us?"

Just then, Ainsley and Mark returned to the room with coasters and tall glasses of mineral water, garnished with lime. Ainsley and Mark shared a flavored mineral water, still in the can. They sat side-by-side on the couch. Both crossed their legs in the same direction, same leg.

"You guys gossiping about me?" Ainsley asked.

"You tell them, sweetheart. She asked me what you said when we told you about the adoption."

"Oh, that." She scrunched up her lips, angled her head, and did a slow neck roll to the left. "The first thing I thought of was that Mom and Dad kidnapped me and that they told me so I could keep their secret in case the police came."

Martel nearly spit out her water. "You're kidding!"

"I thought someone would be very pissed, so I asked them about it. And they told me it was agreed to. I didn't understand it, but I didn't ask again, just in case they were lying to me."

Mark objected, pretending to be offended. "Hey, you really thought we were liars? Seriously, Ainsley?" The skin on his forehead lined as his eyebrows rose.

"I didn't understand how it worked. I didn't—" She stopped herself, creeping on territory that was becoming dangerous, but Martel caught the subtle flavor of her thoughts.

"Because you couldn't understand why anyone would want to give up their own child?" Martel finished for her.

No one spoke or moved.

Martel continued. "You know, Ainsley, I think about that every day. And meeting you here today is my reward. I think I did the right thing, don't you? Your life wouldn't be anything like this. You have the perfect parents, and I can see, they have the perfect daughter."

"Mom says you didn't even tell him. Why did you do that, Martel?"

The use of her name instantly turned something on inside her. Her eyes watered, but she worked to keep them in check without spilling over. Her stomach began to flip-flop. Her parched mouth needed another drink, so she gulped down half the glass.

"Ainsley, I think it would be more appropriate to call her Miss Long. Although, you'll soon be Mrs. Hamlin, right?"

"Yes, in June." She looked at her daughter. "You can call me Martel, whatever you like to call me. I'm not offended by any of it."

The tiny white lie was eating a small hole in her gut, but she could handle it. Lori's tense expression softened. Mark's gaze was deflected, not engaging at all.

"Well, as long as I don't have to call you mom. She's my mom. He's my dad. That won't change, so I'll have to think about it. But you are a teacher, and your kids call you Miss Long, right?"

"To my face, yes. Some call me other names, I'm sure."

Ainsley grinned, showing off one tooth that had turned to the side and would require braces, and soon. Just like Martel had to do as a child.

"Your biological father is Damon Hamlin. I have a picture of the two of us here. Taken in Florida, where we met again and where we are going to get married." She handed the girl the photograph of the two of them at sunset.

Ainsley studied Damon's face. She turned to Mark. "He sorta looks like a blonder version of you, Dad. Should I be expecting another secret here?"

Mark took the photograph, his mouth showing the faint remnants of a curious smile. "I don't see it." Then he turned his head and looked at it from another angle. "Maybe, yeah, maybe a little bit."

He handed the photograph back to Martel.

"It's yours, if you want it, Ainsley. You don't have to accept it, but I planned on giving you a few pictures of our families, if you were curious."

She wrinkled her nose. "No thanks. No offense, but it's kind of creepy looking at people I'm related to and yet don't know. But I'll keep this one." She placed it on the coffee table in front of her, staring down at it.

"Completely understandable," Martel said as she put the other photographs back in her computer case and zipped it up. "My mother is passed, but my dad is still alive. We don't see each other much."

She was instantly annoyed at her comment, as if babbling along would take the gunpowder out of the room. This was starting to be hard. Ainsley's question still stuck in her heart like a fishhook. It was festering.

Ainsley reached for Mark's wrist to check the time. Lori gave her a scowl. Martel was disappointed their meeting might be cut short or Ainsley had lost interest, so she began words she'd rehearsed many times.

"Ainsley, I wanted to just tell you a couple of things, and then I guess you have to be off someplace else. I don't want to keep you or interfere with your life in any way."

"It's okay. We're good. I was just checking. Practice isn't for another hour."

"Okay, great." Martel placed her palms together, bringing her twin third fingers up to her lips and then began again. "When I found out I was pregnant, Damon had already gone off to the Navy, to his training to become a SEAL. You know what a SEAL is?"

"The bad-ass dudes with all the tats."

"Ainsley! That's not very nice!" Lori shouted, her back stiffening.

"Well, I see them on T.V. The movies always show them with full sleeves, muscles." She picked up their picture. "He's got some."

"They are elite military warriors, Ainsley," Mark inserted. "Very, very dangerous work, and only a few can qualify to be on these teams. They've done some incredible things, and we owe them a lot."

"I know that. I wasn't saying—"

"Don't forget to show your respect," Lori whispered.

"So why didn't this war hero come here and face me, huh?" Ainsley's eyes suddenly got angry and red.

"Well, I made the agreement with your parents. We

decided I'd meet you first, and then we'd go from there. I—"

Ainsley was direct, interrupting. "So why didn't you ask to bring him? And where was he all these years?"

It was a question Martel hadn't been prepared for.

"I was young. My intention was never to interfere with your parents, Ainsley."

"But now that he knows, where is he?"

"Because I didn't give him a chance to. He's only learned about you since Christmas. I never told him."

"Why? Don't you think he would want to know?" she asked. Again, her eyes looked like they were about to burst. "You wouldn't like it if it was done to you, right?"

"No. You're right. I tried to find him, but I honestly didn't try very hard. My mind was made up. I was going to give you up for adoption. The most difficult decision I've ever made in my life, but it was the right one, Ainsley. He was off on his deployments and trainings, and when he didn't come look for me, well, I figured he'd moved on. I didn't want to interfere in his life either. But we met again at a wedding, and when we got close again, I told him."

"So was he pissed at you?"

"Ainsley watch your language, please," said Lori Newberg.

"No, the truth is, he was ashamed. He feels he abandoned us both. It's been a difficult thing for him to bear, and I know he still struggles with it." Martel felt her voice quiver and her upper body shake. "I'll be the first to admit, we both know we made some mistakes. Lots of mistakes. But you were not one of them, sweetheart."

That seemed to leave Ainsley without a retort. Satisfied perhaps she'd lowered the pressure a bit, Martel gathered her thoughts carefully. "He asked me to tell you that he loves you, we both love you, and that he agrees I did the right thing by giving you to a loving family who could do all the things we couldn't do, so you could have a life you wouldn't have had with us. He wanted me to tell you we did it because we love you."

Ainsley sat back into the couch, crossing her arms over her chest. Her chin was low, edges of her mouth pointed down, and a worry line appeared at the bridge of her nose. She bit her lip in reflex and then said, "So, what do we do now?" She fussed with her clothes and averted her gaze. "Am I supposed to accept that I have four parents now instead of two?" Before Lori could run over to her, she continued, "What if that's not what *I* want?"

Lori was at her side, hugging her, holding her head against her chest. "Ainsley, sweetheart, I know it's confusing, but no, nothing's changed. Nobody is going to make you do anything. All of our lives stay the same. We'll always be your parents; we love you, and we're raising you. That's not going to change. I'm sorry. Maybe this wasn't a good idea—Mark?"

"It's up to you, kid. You don't ever have to see her again if you don't want to. That's the deal we made with her. You agreed on that basis. I believe her at her word. If that's what you want, that's exactly what you'll get. Miss Long is fine with that. The only one who has any decision to make is you, Ainsley. It's all up to you, and always has been."

"Well, I was curious," she began tentatively, "What kind of a person could have the heart to give their child away. I've thought about you a lot too, Miss Long. Except I didn't look at you in a good way at all. I thought you were some kind of monster. I still don't understand how you could do that. You're nicer than I imagined, but I don't want you to hurt my parents. I don't think I want to do anything to cause that to happen."

Martel was stunned with the truth, the anger in her young soul. It wasn't what she expected, but Damon had warned her. She was about to gather her things and suggest they terminate the meeting when Ainsley added, "I don't think I could ever be friends because I don't trust you." She reached across the table, picked up the picture of the two of them, and handed it back to Martel. "I don't want this. Maybe I will later, but not now."

Ainsley got up and ran upstairs. Martel heard a door slam shut.

And then familiar cold silence surrounded her, her broken heart in freefall.

CHAPTER 7

D AMON GRABBED A burger at the Scupper and joined several others from Team 3. They were inside the back room at the rear of the restaurant, where all the trophy pictures and flags were pinned, sort of the unofficial SEALs of Coronado clubhouse. Several of their members in past classes had spray-painted frog and tadpole pictures on the wall, along with some of the class logos, even class tee shirts were mounted and framed, as well as pictures of various campaigns in countries all over the world. Nothing was labeled or would mean anything to anyone else except those who knew these men by their faces.

He decided to slather his insides with the greasy but delicious fries and the double buffalo burger with extra cheese, along with a long neck, because he wasn't in Martel's company. She'd be horrified at his menu choice.

There was the usual smack talk, teasing someone

who got engaged, someone who had a birthday, or someone who got their wife knocked up. It was low-level talk, mindless, irreverent, and didn't mean the disrespect it might sound to the untrained ear. They used it as a platform for basic communication when they really had nothing important to say. It was just touching and feels on the verbal side.

Several high school hotties swung back around after having spotted them through the open doorway. Probably on a dare, these *too-young* ladies entered their den. One of them asked for their autograph. This kind of fraternization was discouraged, for obvious reasons, so one of the SEALs signed a small notebook as SEAL Team 3 and his name, which wasn't legible. In this way, the girls would leave quickly, without lingering any longer than necessary. It was handled in a way that wasn't rude but curtailed the meeting efficiently so that the appearance of something else was lessened.

But it was a problem. They were always a target. And to those who couldn't help themselves being in the limelight, couldn't help making names for themselves either by writing a tell-all book or going on a bunch of interviews, which also was discouraged, these encounters were mistakes. They were supposed to do the impossible—be invisible. But everyone had an opinion and a story about SEALs, so everyone clamored for their attention.

If he wanted to, Damon could go around posing or boasting about things he never did.

That disgusted him.

So it was back to the low-level smack talk.

"I understand Libby and the cheerleaders made you some Save The Date cards. How come you're not passing them around, you dork?" one of the newbies asked Damon.

"As a matter of fact,"—he pulled out one card and handed it to Cooper—"none of you assholes are invited."

That bought him some scorn. Coop examined the card, winked, and put it in his pocket. "We'll try," he mouthed across the table. "So Martel's back in Florida?" he then asked.

"Not sure, actually." Damon checked his phone. "I should hear any minute how the meeting went. You know, the meeting?"

Cooper nodded and sipped his ice water. He'd eaten all his lettuce and tomato and half his garden burger, served dry as toast, but none of the bread. He had a few sweet potato fries—toasted, not deep fried—left on his plate, and Damon grabbed one. It tasted like cardboard.

"Even when Libby's not around, you still eat like this?" he said to the team's lead medic.

"Hey, I'm the reason the family eats this way. It

starts with me. Libby would have one of your buffalo burgers if it were left up to her, smeared an inch thick with mayonnaise." He tossed a fry in his mouth and wiggled his eyebrows. "But I got her trained." His eyes sparkled.

The rest of the younger SEALs, most of them single, added some very disrespectful comments to that. It had been a challenge all during dinner to see who could pose the best one-liner.

Fredo was sitting next to Coop. "No lie, Damon, Coop here knows about this shit. You want to have children? You start eating tofu and drinking gallons of water. I'm living proof of that."

Damon had heard the story of how Fredo had been despondent to learn he was sterile, and he had hidden it from his wife. Cooper had put him on a health regimen, and all of a sudden, Mia got pregnant with twins. It seemed to have reversed his sterility problem. The two SEALs were best friends but a very mismatched pair.

He didn't say it, but Damon knew he didn't have a sterility problem. Coop sent him a wink of understanding.

All of a sudden, all their phones vibrated or pinged, which meant something was up, and it was an emergency. Damon checked the message.

Emergency deployment in one hour. Team 3 building.

Urgent DTI looking for volunteers. Please respond and then present if available.

Damon pushed the confirmation letter "C" and saw Coop had done the same. It was never optional for the medic or for Fredo, but some from their team might be with family for the Valentine holiday, and it sounded like they wanted a small group.

"Adios, Amigos," Coop said, standing, pulling up his khakis. "Duty calls."

Fredo, Damon, and several others stood as well and left the others to finish their beers.

"Hey, Coop, I got my girl coming in tomorrow from Connecticut," said one of the tadpoles. "Tell Kyle, okay?"

"Not a problem, but that's your story to tell. You go be with your girl. You need a full rotation to go on these, because they're not training missions, froglet," Coop said, patting the young SEAL's shoulder.

As they exited the Scupper and headed for their vehicles, Damon asked the two of them, "So it's Mexico, is it?"

"I'm guessing. Kelly Fielding and Ridgeway left yesterday. I'm thinking they got into some trouble. But it's just a guess," Coop whispered. "You didn't hear it from me."

"Got it. And holy shit. See you in a few," signed off Damon as he ran for Monica, his bright blue Hummer.

BY THE TIME he hit the Team 3 building with all his gear, he felt like he'd been running for the last hour straight. He'd already sweat through his fatigues. He liked to travel in those because they were indestructible, and sometimes they rode in transports that were drafty with uncomfortable seating arrangements. It was sometimes good to have an extra layer covering his lower limbs, and if he messed them up, they were easy to replace.

But he still hadn't heard from Martel. He decided he'd better give her a call.

Her voice was shaky when she answered.

"Hey there, so you're still standing. How was it?" He pushed his more optimistic side out first so his annoyance with her lack of contact didn't seep through. This was something he'd had to learn the hard way.

"It didn't go very well. I was trying to sort my thoughts before I called you. I've been crying for the past two hours."

Oh shit. Just what we need right now.

"Look, Martel, I'm really sorry to break this to you, but I'm off on an emergency run, so I'll be sort of MIA on you. Anything you need?"

"How long?"

"I have no idea. Hopefully not long. This isn't our regular workup. Something special."

She caught the implication. "I'm sorry I didn't—"

"Look, I got no time for this, honey. Sorry, but have to go. Just give me a brief rundown if you can. I've only got a minute or so before they call the meeting."

This was the bad thing about their quick deployments. They never came at opportune times, and they hadn't had much time to prepare, except they were training all the time between deployments.

"She got angry at me, Damon. She refused all the pictures. I guess I didn't handle it very well."

"Was there an argument?"

"No. She just had an attitude."

"Well, of course she would. Wouldn't you?"

"I was expecting—" Martel broke off in a sigh then a sniffle.

"Fantasyland. I told you about that. Hurts, doesn't it?"

"Yes, you did. I still walked right into it."

"She's got a right to feel how she feels. She'll either get over it or not. But you did what you wanted to do, right?"

"I guess."

"Come on, Martel, you didn't expect her to say, *'Oh, mama! So happy to see you at last!'* Right? I mean, come on. Give her some slack. But don't lie to yourself and don't lie to me, Martel. You did what you wanted. We don't have any right to anything else. You know that."

There was silence on the other end. This sucked all to hell and back a dozen times.

"Say something, please." He knew she'd beat herself up if she didn't and he got injured. Now her mood was infecting him, dammit.

"I don't like accepting that, but you are right. And I got to tell her we both loved her. She got to hear that. Maybe she didn't want to. Maybe that's what triggered it. Finally meeting me and hearing that we gave her up out of love. But I didn't lose it until I got back into my car and got down the end of the block so the Newbergs didn't see me. They apologized for her, but I told them I understood."

"I think you did perfect, sweetheart." He meant it. Martel was the bravest woman he'd met. "Just don't go telling yourself fairy tales, unless it's about my performance in bed, okay?"

Martel chuckled at that. "Right. I can do that all day and night long."

"You better. I'm sure going to be doing that."

"So I'm at the airport, heading back to Florida this afternoon. I changed my plans. I wanted to get out of here, so I'll be home late tonight Florida time, but way earlier than the red eye. I have some messages from my administrator I'm afraid to listen to, but I'll do it on the plane. Just wanted you to know."

"Awesome. I like you being back in Florida. Take a nice long walk on the beach for me. Go have banana pancakes and a good strong cappuccino. I'll call you when I can. We'll be in a different time zone but not sure which one. Love you, sweetheart."

"Love you back. Thanks for calling me. I needed to hear your voice. I didn't want to bring you down."

"No, that's what I'm here for. I'll tell you if it's a problem, trust me. You gotta lean on your team. That's the way we do it. No feeling lonely by yourself. You're part of the team, my team now, and we do this together. That's how it works. That's how we get through all this."

"I know. God, I miss you."

"Well, you could have stayed for Crissakes!"

"I know."

"You did your job. That part to be continued. Something tells me she'll reach out, if they let her. But it's out of our hands right now. You do see that, don't you?"

"I do."

The meeting was beginning.

"Have to go. Love you."

He was forced to hang up before he heard her response. He turned off one switch and turned on another. His attention was laser-focused on the mission in front of them and what part he would be playing.

Coop had been right. Kelly Fielding and Special Agent Ridgeway were missing, feared captured by the cartel they'd been sent to negotiate safe passage with so they could lead a team to apprehend a rival cartel leader later. She'd probably gone down there with tons of cash from Uncle Sam.

Damon guessed it wasn't enough. The cartels, all of them, were getting very rich already from Uncle Sam, the Mexican government, and the poor people being delivered inside the United States in the hundreds.

Things had changed, and the stakes had just gotten higher.

He settled down on the transport plane headed to Baja, adjusted his headset so he could listen to Margaritaville music, used his duty bag as a pillow, and tried to sleep.

They numbered ten, and a lot was expected of them. He'd been told it was probably one of the most dangerous missions he'd ever be on, a fact he neglected to tell Martel.

CHAPTER 8

A T THE AIRPORT, Martel listened to the first of three messages from her school administrator, Carlton Greene.

'Martel, we have a situation here, and I know you are in California for the Valentine's weekend, but I need you to call me back when you get a chance. I'm getting some pushback from a local attorney, and I need your input, if you don't mind.'

The second message was a bit stronger and came in about two hours later, which was late last night, very late for him in Florida.

'Martel, this is Administrator Greene again. I'd like to schedule a time before you return so I can speak to you. I have some questions, and as I said before, I know you are busy, but I'm running into something and need your urgent help. Please give me a call at your earliest convenience.'

And in the third one, which came in early this

morning, Greene sounded near desperate. *I'm going to simply insist I get a call back, Martel. We may be facing a full-scale lawsuit against the school, and you may also be, personally. So that things don't spin out of control, I have to have your cooperation or other steps will be taken.*'

That sounded like a threat.

She kicked herself for not checking her phone before the flight to San Jose today, but she'd been preoccupied, after all.

"Carlton Greene," he said when she dialed his number, picking up before the second ring.

"I'm sorry I wasn't able to return your call, Mr. Greene. I boarded a plane this morning, and then was in a meeting. How—"

He interrupted her. "The Gibbs family have retained a lawyer, and he's making all sorts of threats against me, against the school, and against you. I want to avoid the publicity, but he's demanding I set a meeting up with the both of us tomorrow first thing. I suspect he needs to serve papers, too, but he doesn't need us to do that. He's a bigshot, personal injury attorney from Tampa. I don't like his tone nor his tactics. He *came over to my house last night!*"

"Oh, gee. I'm so sorry."

"I told him you were out of town this weekend, but he insisted on coming over, even interrupting a nice

Valentine's dinner with my wife. The guy is a real jerk, a grandstander. Don't quote me, but I want to get my ducks in a row before we make too many waves and before I have to call the District counsel's office."

"I don't understand. What's the complaint?"

"He claims their daughter has been bullied, harassed. It's a sexual harassment issue now. That as a school district, and you in particular, didn't protect their Cora, and so she'd been sexually assaulted on campus. I guess you got pretty graphic with them."

"Well, I did tell them what I saw and why I was calling for the conference. As far as specifics, I don't have any specifics except what I could see from a distance."

"He wants assault charges brought against the boys. He wants names. Claims we're trying to cover up the abuse by blaming the parents. He says that now they feel like victims too."

"But that's absurd."

"You did call the sheriff's office, right?"

"I did. I spoke to a young lady—I have the name back in my office. They were going to go out and interview the parents and the girl. Do you know, did that happen?" Martel asked.

"Apparently they refused to let the interview take place. They called their lawyer instead. Said you admitted she was assaulted on campus. I guess you did say that."

"Well, they challenged me in my opinion that she'd been exhibiting certain behaviors—"

"Yeah, I know. I know exactly what they're going to go after. Well, can you make a nine o'clock meeting if I can get our counsel there?"

"Sure. You'll have to call a sub for my class. I don't have the list here."

"That's no problem. We're already covering that. But you'll have to contact your union rep."

"My *union* rep? What for?"

"You're gonna need to get representation. Separate from the school district, your own attorney to represent you. Your union does that or will make recommendations."

"Nobody is going to be open today. It's Sunday. I think maybe you should hold the meeting after school. That would give us time to get our ducks in a row."

"Well, there's an issue with that. The other side probably doesn't want us prepared. But they're saying they don't want you teaching Cora's class tomorrow, endangering other students. I think he's going to be going after you personally, Martel."

She was going to be sick. Nothing like this had ever happened to her, nor to anyone she knew. "Endangering other students? Really? I was trying to let them know about that incident, not hiding it. I wanted them to seek counseling for her and gave them the courtesy of a heads-up before the sheriff or Child Protective Services showed up at their front door."

"I know. We discussed all this before you had your meeting. I didn't see this possibility. Wish I had."

That brought up another question. "So will I be placed on administrative leave then?"

"Possibly. I have to wait and see what counsel says."

Her spotless reputation was already trashed in her own mind. The upset over her meeting with Ainsley this morning was a distant second to this one. For the first time, she began to question whether or not she'd have a job after today. It might even become something of a criminal nature, although she doubted it.

"I'll be boarding in about an hour. I get in at ten, and by the time I get home, it will be close to midnight. You just call me with the where and when of the meeting, and I'll spend my minutes here right now and see if I can get in touch with the union. And, Mr. Greene, I'm so sorry for all this. I still think we made the right call. This wasn't the reaction I was anticipating when I spoke to them on Friday. When they left, they were totally focused on their daughter, or so it appeared. I was proud of how they were handling it as a couple. I even—"

Martel stopped mid-sentence.

"What?"

"I gave them my cell phone number and asked them to call anytime over the weekend if something came up. They planned on keeping Cora home on Monday. I wonder if the visit from the sheriff's department went badly."

"That's a question for counsel, if they can get that." Greene sighed. There was an extra weight to his concern. "If they go after you, they'll dig into everything. Everyone has something in their closet. Whatever it is, if this goes into a full trial situation, everything about your past will be on public view."

He was sounding like a man who had a past, Martel thought.

In any case, she certainly had one. And that would definitely alter the odds of any chance she'd have a relationship with Ainsley or her adoptive parents going forward, and even that was a stretch. Her move to San Diego might be seen as her running away from some painful chapter for her in Florida, a gross mischaracterization.

But it could happen.

The timing was so wrong. Damon was gone. What a thing to drag him through when he returned. How would she be able to explain it to him?

She needed someone in her corner who could defang the aggressive Tampa attorney.

Her call to her union representative went to voice

mail, of course. She tried to call Kaitlyn but didn't get an answer. She and her new husband, Greg, had gone to Disney World, and she wasn't going to be back in class until Wednesday.

So she called Aimee Carr, the wife of Andy, who had served with Damon on SEAL Team 3 and now lived in Sunset Beach.

Grateful she didn't ask too many questions, Aimee suggested she might have someone who could assist her in getting someone good. But she'd need until tomorrow.

There was no one else to call. With Damon and Kaitlyn gone, her mother passed, and her father more or less MIA, Martel was all alone.

Then she thought about Gran Karmody, the attorney who helped her set up the meeting with Ainsley. He was a grandfatherly type of old cuss and perhaps not as sleazy as it sounded like the Gibbs' attorney was, but he could be just the right kind of sly.

There was so much riding on this, she hesitated to call him, but did leave a message, finally. "I'm flying home tomorrow from my meeting with my daughter. She's beautiful, Mr. Karmody. But now it seems I have another unrelated problem. I need you to help me find someone who can represent me. Call me and we can talk."

That was all she could do, she thought as she

boarded the plane for Tampa. She settled in her seat, looking out at the blue sky of San Jose, so close to where she'd been raised. Was she leaving California or going home? No answer came to mind as the plane took off, soaring into the air above San Francisco Bay, before taking a sharp turn inland, crossing over green valleys, orchards in the distance, the San Joaquin valley breadbasket, and beyond.

What if all the mistakes of her past became public gossip? She'd agreed to own up to all this, to move forward, learn from these mistakes, and create a compelling future with Damon.

But she never anticipated this. This had the potential to follow her all the way across country, affect her ability to work in California, do anything anywhere. It was like having to wear a scarlet letter. She'd be gobbled up in the social media explosion that was surely coming. She could even see the headline in the Tampa Bay Times,

Local Pinellas County teacher accused of abuse.

She was about to find out how strong she was and who her real friends and allies were.

CHAPTER 9

WHEN THE TRANSPORT landed at the former military base in Baja, it was still dark outside. These big behemoths were so loud that any planning or discussions were futile. The group who went consisted of Kyle, their LPO, Coop, Tucker, Trace, Jason, Fredo, Armando, Danny, T.J., and him. Jameson Daniels elected not to go because his wife was due to deliver any day. It was a good mix, with communications specialists, snipers, explosive experts, a drone specialist, two native Spanish speakers, and most of their most senior members.

They were transported to an abandoned housing project along the Sea of Cortez, a half hour bumpy ride from Cabo San Lucas, just outside of LaPaz. The project was part of a new resort that had bankrupted before the rest of the infrastructure and town itself were created. Grand vistas of the ocean and Mexican lands beyond were plentiful in the long view, but many of the thoroughfares that were to be four-laned expressways were reduced to two lanes and often only one. Night travel was extremely hazardous, and the vans carrying the team snaked around potholes and piles of abandoned construction equipment and materials at a very slow pace.

But what was problematic for their arrival was also a barrier for many of the locals, and it isolated the team from the curious. While they were led to believe the road between the project and Cabo San Lucas, as well as Todos Santos, were not bad, many of them were dirt.

The completed building was three stories with a great hall/dining room on the main floor. The new condos, beautifully floored in glistening white marble, were above the ground floor. Between the ten of them, they were allowed use of the entire second and third floors, nearly fifteen suites.

Since the ownership of the land reverted back to the governor of the state of Baja California Sur, posing as potential buyers gave them a wide berth with little interference. Local staff were "borrowed" from the governor's resort on the mainland, oddly enough, so the prospective purchasers could have "the full ownership experience." If it was suspected these men were Navy SEALs, no one indicated such.

They traveled on their own with no escort, merely

three rotating drivers who were undercover regular Navy Spanish speakers, running errands and transporting them by van. Their "fishing equipment" was stowed in surplus Coast Guard duty boxes from the seventies, long used by commercial fishermen in the San Diego area. They were a perfect disguise for some of their explosives and fire power, and the drivers, being military themselves, knew how to handle them.

A banker's box of real estate contracts and pro forma reports were provided, even including parcel maps and descriptions of the project itself. But most of the paperwork they brought were props to justify their cover, intended to calm the wagging tongues of the cook and maintenance staff. Kyle indicated they suspected a few of them would be plants, people who would report directly to the governor.

They were instructed to bunk in pairs. One large suite was designated as the equipment room. The lock on the door was quickly switched out to a keyless entry utilizing a combination code that noted date and time of access. Everyone's entrance and exit recorded with a camera Fredo installed inside the unit and one placed in the hallway outside the door.

He'd brought several other keyless pads and promised to get them working later that morning sometime.

There was only time for a quick team meeting over a buffet of fresh fruits, cold fish, lukewarm rice and beans and corn tortillas—a breakfast none of them had on a regular basis. One thing sorely missed was beer, so that was at the top of the sticky note hung in the kitchen. Cans of juice and bottled waters filled the one of the kitchen refrigerators.

When the prep staff left, Kyle spread out some maps and surveillance posters taken the day before when the mission had been approved.

"Carter Ridgeway and Kelly Fielding are being held at the Quantos Villa Ascension, home of the C.A.Sur or, as the DEA guys call them, California Surf Club, a relatively new cartel to form here in Baja. It's a large complex, heavily gated and armed twenty-four seven, with about five acres of lush landscaping and pools and cottages tucked away here and there. From the air, it masquerades as a tropical Mexican paradise with villas for wealthy tourists. Indeed, at one time, it was one of the most exclusive resorts on the west coast of Mexico. It's location to the mainland, as well as close proximity to the open sea of the Pacific Ocean, make it ideal for smuggling people and contraband in and out. They have a fleet of very fast pleasure boats. Some of them can outrun our Coasties."

The team studied the aerial photographs taken by drone.

"We spotted Kelly sitting outside a bungalow smoking a cigarette only once. Unbeknownst to their captors, both Kelly and Carter have embedded microchips which they can turn off and on with the touch of a finger to signal something. We get a weak signal from Ridgeway but clear on the other side of the complex, which makes sense. He may be being held in a metal shipping container, which could interfere with the transmission. We don't know if he's being tortured, but we do know they've both spotted groups of mostly male runners held in a secured lockdown location. They managed to get that information out before their capture."

"How do you know they're runners? You mean people being assisted to cross the border?" asked Jason.

"There are all kinds of human trafficking. Some pay a fee to be taken across the border, but others gain their freedom by carrying narcotics in their body cavities, their families back home being watched and held hostage until the mission is accomplished. Many of these will then release into the interior of the U.S. or come back down to help pay for another family member's passage, when they do it all over again, this time with their little sister or their mother or grandmother.

"They're like slaves, and the cartels pick them up in remote locations and drop them off similarly. Pickups are timed. If someone doesn't make their rendezvous, they're done. There's a high turnover, and nearly twenty percent of these don't survive the trip."

"So all this stems from this location?" asked Danny.

"This is one of hundreds all over Mexico. They own ranches and houses in California, Texas, Montana, and even Idaho where the drugs are stored and then distributed all over the U.S. There's so much demand that turf wars in the states are not heard of much. Turf wars in Mexico, now that's another thing."

"This location is where they pick up the drugs for land-based entries then. Is that right?" asked Damon.

"Yes. There are other warehouses near the marinas. It's such a lucrative venture that they can pose as wealthy Mexican and European tourists or landowners because they *are* wealthy landowners. They make billions. We have jokers coming all the way over here from the Middle East, direct from the poppy planta-tions and Kush regions to participate. It's a criminal conspiracy, partnership, and organization stronger than most governments. This cartel is only one of dozens. And Uncle Sam works with some of them. In fact, we've worked with this one before when they've helped us with some terrorist watch group individuals that slipped through our borders. They aren't exactly friendly with these groups, so they gladly take our money and help us catch them. Until yesterday. Yesterday, they moved from being an ally, admittedly a dangerous and not totally trustworthy ally, to being an enemy. Kelly and Carter walked right into it."

"What's the plan, Kyle?" asked Cooper. "How are you going to get around these armed guards?"

"That's a pretty big area for only ten of us," added T.J.

"We start a fire. Gentlemen, we're going to blow up one of their buildings, and it's going to be so big we're going to need a huge water tanker truck, rescue vehicles, and a boatload of crew to put it out." Kyle grinned.

"Do you happen to have one of those tankers?" asked Damon.

"We sure do. It's stored in that incomplete fire station right over there." Kyle pointed to the distinctive red brick building with large rollup bay doors. "And we think, given a large-enough emergency, they might run over here and commandeer this unit. Maybe ask for some manpower."

Damon was confused.

"I think we'll let them do it. And if not, well, we'll drive it over to them and offer our services."

They were released at dawn to get a couple of hours of sleep before they would go on their first rounds of exploratory. This would also give Kyle time to update his intel by calling the commander back in Coronado, just in case something had changed. Coop approached Kyle, with Damon right behind him, asking a question.

"You got tools here somewhere? I'm thinking I

should maybe make sure that thing works out there or we'll be caught with our pants down around our ankles and no bride in sight."

"Whoa. That's an image I won't get out of my head anytime soon. But I get your point. Excellent idea. You feel like tickling her insides a bit?"

"Just wanna be sure. Depends on how long she's been standing. We're close to the ocean, salt water, you get the drill."

"Say no more. God, I'm glad I brought you!" Kyle shook his hand and sent him on his way.

Before Kyle could get distracted elsewhere, Damon asked him a burning question.

"You didn't say anything about our cells. Are we allowed?" he asked.

"You bet. This time, the gear isn't that sophisticated for that kind of stuff. Unless you have 'Badass Navy SEAL' all over your FB page or phone description, and you better not because that'll get you tossed, you're good."

"Thanks, Kyle." Damon headed for the stairs. "Oh, and Martel said she missed seeing Christy at the bonfire. She liked it."

"Oh, yeah? She fitting in already?"

"I think so, sir. But you know women. I mean, how do you ever know for sure?"

"Indeed, I do, Damon. Strangest, most beautiful

creatures on this planet. Make you work so hard, hurt so hard, and want so hard. You're kicking and screaming and loving every minute of it. Guys who don't get that don't get loved."

No truer words were ever spoken. "Spoken by one who I'm sure is."

"Thanks, Damon. Now you go get some rest, and we'll talk later. I understand she went to visit your little girl. I'd like to hear about it sometime. And tell the guys about the phones, 'cause I forgot to."

"Yessir." Damon was surprised Kyle knew about Martel's trip to Palo Alto but figured nothing much passed between the four amigos, as they were called: Kyle, Coop, Fredo, and Armando. All four pillars of the same fortress they called their platoon at SEAL Team 3.

Upstairs, he informed the other rooms about the cell phone use and entered his own. Jason had requested they room together since they were both about the same time on the teams, and they also had some adventures in Florida.

The suite was huge, each equipped with a king-sized bed. Jason sat with his cell phone in his lap.

"Pretty cool, isn't it?" the heavily inked Pacific Islander said, gesturing at the suite. "Heard you were talking about phones. Figured I'd get the scoop first before I go opening up a can of worms."

"Have at it. I'm going to."

He entered his room and partially closed the bedroom door, leaving a good foot-wide opening, then dialed Martel. He'd been concerned ever since her disturbing phone call. He willed himself to calm down as he waited for the rings.

But it went straight to voicemail.

"Hey, Babe. We're here, all safe and sound. I'm going to hit the sack for a couple of winks, and then we'll be on our way, exploring this *project*," he said with emphasis. "Nice weather so far. Not sure how available I'll be today, but keep trying and be sure to reach out to Christy or someone if you need help. I'm serious about that. Don't do stuff alone. You're pretty strong, but there comes a time when it all starts feeling like too much, and you just gotta step away and get some help."

Then he thought about something else. "You might give Lizzie Daniels a call, so you can let us know how if the baby's coming. Jameson stayed behind. I think you knew he'd do that."

He wrinkled his brow and finished up. "Love you, and wish you were here. The water is blue, and I've got this killer view and room. Jason is a poor substitute for the love of my life. Take care, be good, get some help if you're overwhelmed, and don't ever forget that I love you. More every day. You did good this morning, Martel. Everything will be okay. You'll see. Bye."

He hoped she'd find some comfort in his words, but he was always nervous about leaving long voicemails. It increased the chances that he would say something that would be taken the wrong way.

Kyle was right. Women were so complicated but incredible creatures. He wanted to feel that love from her forever.

CHAPTER 10

MARTEL PULLED UP to her rental and grabbed her suitcase. She noted people were putting their cans out for the early morning pickup, so she left her suitcase by her front door and struggled with the two plastic bins. One of them had a broken wheel, and it just wouldn't budge. She nearly toppled it.

"Hey, hey, let me get this, miss."

He was an older guy, maybe ten years older than her, with salt and pepper beard and hair, extremely handsome.

"Thank you," she said as he pulled the cans out of her grip. She waited for him to place them at the street.

"You just getting back?" he asked, noting her suit-case.

"Yes, a little Valentine's Day trip."

He nodded his head, hand over his mouth. "I'm your new neighbor, Carl Frame. I just bought the duplex next door. Going to be working on it."

She shook his hand. "I'm Martel," and left it at that. Placing her hand on the pull up grip, she thanked him again. "It's been a long day, so I'm going to crash."

He waved at her and began to walk away. "I'll take a raincheck."

It was an odd comment. She didn't owe him anything. But when she turned, he'd already gone.

She double checked all the doors and windows then checked her phone and saw she'd missed a call from Damon. She started listening to it when her phone rang.

"Hey there, little lady. Howz it going these days?" Martel was so happy to hear the lawyer's familiar southern accent, relieved he cared enough to call her at night.

"Mr. Karmody, thank you so much for calling. I didn't expect you until tomorrow."

"Well, I can't resist a pretty woman. You sounded a little stressed. Glad it wasn't too late. I considered that."

"No. This is better, much better."

"Normally, I like to have you come into my office, and we can have a proper chat, but I imagine you have school tomorrow, so try to be brief and how can I help you?"

"I'm not sure if you can. I mean, I don't know if you do that kind of law."

"What kind of law?"

"I might be sued for sexual abuse or just abuse or failure to watch out for one of my students."

"Holy cow. You don't mess around with little things, do you? How could something like that happen?"

"Well, I noticed something on campus a few days ago, and I wanted to report it to the sheriff. I'm *required* to report it, I should say. One of my students, a girl, was doing pre-sexual things, allowing things to be done to her."

"Missy, there's no such thing as pre-sexual in the eyes of the law. It's either sexual or not sexual. If it's even a little bit sexual, it's sexual. Get my drift?"

"I do, sir."

"And she was doing something with another girl or a boy?"

"Two boys."

"And what were they doing?"

"She was consensually, or it appeared to be consensual anyway, letting them touch her in her underwear, her panties."

"I see. And was there any penetration?"

"Oh god, I have no idea. I was clear across the yard. I don't think it could be. I don't think the boys knew what they were doing, but it looked like Cora—she's my student—did. And before I reported it to the authorities, and after checking with my administrator, I asked for a parent conference and met with them both on Friday after school."

"Okay. And what was the result?"

"Well, at first the mother had a complete defensive attitude. I told them that, to me, she exhibited adult behavior, and that, based on my training as a teacher and counselor, was a learned behavior, probably taught to her by an older person, man or woman. They didn't like hearing that or hearing what she was allowing the boys to do. I didn't get any indication it was against her will, but I just wanted someone to look into it, and I wanted them not to be blindsided by the sheriff coming to their front door."

"Okay. And this is normally the way it's handled?"

"We don't have a way it's handled. I relied on my administrator. He didn't ask to be part of the conversation. I told him what I thought was the right thing to do, and he agreed, so I set up the appointment."

"Well, now it's two against one as far as what you said and what they said or did. So now they're coming after you? Just why is that?"

"They've hired an attorney in Tampa and are treating it like she was raped on campus and neither me nor the school did anything to stop it and, in fact, encouraged it by not stopping it. I can see why they think that, but that wasn't the purpose of the meeting."

"Well, your administrator didn't do you any favors, but did the sheriff go to the house?"

"No one would let them in. And they're blaming me for that, too, like I damaged their reputation because the car came to the house, making all their neighbors think something wrong had happened."

"Fact of the matter is, something wrong probably did happen to her, from the sounds of it. But it's odd that they reacted that way. Who did they hire?"

"I'm sorry. I don't have all the information. My administrator said it was some personal injury attorney with a billboard on the freeway. He called me when I was up visiting with Damon and Ainsley, my daughter. Today, I got to meet her for the first time, Mr. Karmody."

"Oh, that's wonderful. How did that go? I'll bet she's so smart."

Martel hesitated, suddenly overcome with tears. With her lower lip quivering, she tried to get out, "Oh, not so well. She got angry with me. I jumped right from that into finding out about this attorney who's coming after me, so it's not been one of my better days."

She sniffled and found tissues to blow her nose.

"You poor dear. Are you still in California?"

"No, I'm back at my house. Just got in. Damon's on a deployment, an emergency."

"So you have that, too."

"I feel like a deer in the headlights. They don't want me in class. The attorney is demanding a morning meeting—"

"Wait a minute. Who doesn't want you in class?"

"The attorney said I shouldn't be around children because I don't do a good job of protecting them. My administrator agreed and has already gotten me a sub. I'm to meet with this attorney, and I don't know what to do."

"Your admin isn't doing you any favors. He's giving off the aura of guilt, like a no-confidence vote. Do you get along well with him?"

"Yes, we're fine. But he let something slip when he was talking to me, and I picked up on a weird vibe. He commented about them digging up dirt from our past and that social media could get heated and cruel. I just got the impression he had an issue he was wanting to hide. Not about Cora or anything at the school but from his past, perhaps a long time ago. Again, this is just a hunch."

"Kind of makes sense. Now, if you were to guess, who would you say has taught Cora these things? Do you think it's the father? They're usually the suspects. Is this his natural child?"

"I don't know, honestly, but I think she is. They look alike. He just doesn't seem like someone who would do that. But how would I know? They had a minor argument about her family. He was sort of pointing the finger at them, for some reason. The mother told him not to harm them, and I thought that was odd. The mom is kind of a mess, but the father seems hard working, a little depressed, but otherwise okay. She's on a downward spiral."

"If anyone asks you about her, keep your mouth shut, please."

"Sure. No problem. You mean I shouldn't have—"

"No, only thing you did wrong was not have your admin with you during the conference. But if he didn't insert himself or volunteer it, that can't be blamed on you. You were the one who called him first, I take it?"

"Yes. I told him, and then we agreed I'd talk to the parents and inform them. Together."

"You and the admin together?"

"No, I would talk to the parents together, not one at a time."

"Gotcha." He sighed and then posed another question. "Why are you worried about your past? You have nothing to hide."

"My daughter. Giving up my daughter for adoption. That wouldn't look very good if it came out in a lawsuit, would it?"

"There's no reason it would. Besides, the adoption was handled in Oregon. I don't think they'd know where to look. You haven't told anyone, have you?"

Martel's spirits collapsed again. It was getting so difficult to talk. "Only several of the wives on SEAL Team 3, my friend here who's also married to a SEAL. But not anyone else."

"These fellas are based in San Diego?"

"Yes."

"How big is SEAL Team 3?"

"Oh, I don't know the exact number, but I think about two hundred. Their platoon is much smaller, thirty-five or so. Maybe fifty. I don't know."

"I want you to stop talking about it, Martel. Especially with that administrator. I don't like what I'm hearing about him. Is it a him or her?"

"Him. He's very nice. I've never had any problems with him. Always very supportive of the teachers. I've done a good job of keeping that one to myself."

"Except for fifty or so men on SEAL Team 3 and their wives, maybe their children if they were listening. You see where I'm going?"

"Yes," she croaked, barely able to get it out. "I'm such an idiot."

"No, you're not an idiot, but there are a lot of things that could get sticky if not handled properly. We have to control the narrative. Usually, guilty people try to do that, like on TV. In your case, your past isn't indicative of who you are today. You didn't do anything wrong. You admittedly made a mistake, and I'll wager you've paid a high price for that."

"I have." She was tired, wanted to take a hot shower and just peel herself into bed. "Mr. Karmody, I'm exhausted. So, before I literally fall asleep on the phone, does this sound like something you'd be able to help me with? Or can you give me the name of someone else who could?"

"I think so. Your union should help, but you don't want them using their attorneys, even though they'll try to convince you of it. We can all work together. But I'm thinking about a lady I know who just salivates to go against attorneys like this gentleman you described, the ones who make a huge case out of a misunderstanding and cost everyone enormous sums of money, all for greed. But she's about as sharp as they come."

"So you'll call her then, or do I have to do it tomorrow?"

"You let me know what time your meeting is and where, and I'll make sure we both show up. If she can't, because I don't know anything about her schedule, I'll come. But I'm pretty sure she'll want to be there."

"You don't know how relieved that makes me feel."

"Well, we've got some homework to do. We need to find out who is doing the abuse, the source of it. If that comes out, I have a feeling this little ball of yarn will untangle itself."

"Wouldn't that be nice? Oh, thank you!"

"You go take your shower and turn in. I'll talk to you in the morning. Don't forget to let me know when the meeting is first thing."

"I promise. Thanks so much. I know this probably isn't something you do every day, but I just appreciate having someone on my side I can trust."

"Of course. And I don't take on any clients I don't believe in, either. If I'm not convinced they are innocent, I don't get involved. This shouldn't be happening to you. I want to help you fix it."

"How much will this cost?"

"If we have to hire a private detective, it could be sizeable. We'll cross that bridge when we come to it. The bottom line is you're innocent, and we just have to do what we can to prove it."

After the call, she hesitated to listen to Damon's message but decided she needed that little bit of extra support. She took her shower, sat down on the couch overlooking the silver moonlight-created crystals of the calm bay this evening, and pressed play.

'Love you, and wish you were here. The water is blue, and I've got this killer view and room. Jason is a poor substitute for the love of my life. Take care, be good, get some help if you're overwhelmed, and don't ever forget that I love you. More every day. You did good this morning, Martel. Everything will be okay. You'll see. Bye.'

CHAPTER 11

THE TEAM WAS dropped off in two locations just outside Cabo San Lucas and were to rendezvous back in two hours. The location of the villa could be seen from downtown, nestled into foothills overlooking the lower part of the peninsula and Sea of Cortez. With specialized scopes, anyone up on the hillside would be able to see the faces of people below, so their vantage point to spot for operations against them was excellent.

But Coop had brought his drones, including one for use at night that could detect heat signatures. It wasn't as sophisticated as the ones the Feds were using, but they were smaller and could get in and out without detection since they were nearly silent. If they launched one, they were required to report it so there wasn't a mid-air accident, which had happened when there were too many operators with too many toys.

Damon was in Coop's group while the other four

men went with Kyle into town from the other side.

"You make it look like you're just flying a little toy," Damon said as he watched the drone take off.

"Yeah, I don't think they use them much down here. That probably won't last, though. With the money they're making, they'll eventually set up a death drone system to keep out airspace intruders. But you never know. Sometimes, these guys fool you."

"That's the truth," agreed Damon.

"So you're gonna program it to just do circle reconnaissance?" asked Fredo.

"Yup."

Fredo explained earlier that they'd take the drone up to high altitude and then send it over the site before lowering it for a closer look. That way, the villa wouldn't know it was coming.

"I'll send the recording to the Feds so they can help with the analysis," said Coop.

"So when's the barbeque?" asked Jason.

Damon, Coop and Fredo chuckled.

"We'll see what she brings home. If it was me, I'd want it tonight. But we gotta know where we're going first."

"I don't like the idea of Kelly and Ridgeway being up there longer either," said Damon.

Fredo asked Coop another question. "Did Kyle say there had been any random demands for either of them?"

"Not sure. I haven't heard."

Coop's little plane had completely disappeared into the clouds overhead, but he still had a bird's eye view on his monitor. He scanned the horizon in front and then casually took a peek behind him.

"Jason and Damon, you guys act interested in rocks or something. Go look at that stone wall. Touch the soil. Let me know if anyone is watching me and this bird," asked Coop.

Both of them fanned out, scraping and tapping the ground like they were combing for shells at the beach. Damon did find several .38 casings and a red shotgun shell. They were about ten minutes outside of the beginnings of the outskirts of Cabo. "Probably a great place to do some target practice," he said.

"Kinda dumb, though. The whole place would hear it," said Fredo.

"Got anybody interested?" Coop asked over his shoulder. He tapped on his monitor a couple of times and shook his head.

"Not a soul," responded Jason.

"Nobody close by anyway," added Damon.

Coop tapped on the monitor again and then swore. Damon and Jason came running back to his side to ask what was wrong.

"So we're gonna act real disappointed here, because

we just lost our little plane, okay?"

"Did you?" asked Jason.

"What does that look like?" Coop showed him the view of the complex, looking like a bunch of orange Monopoly houses clustered together with a large pool in the rear surrounded by a freeform lawn, smaller sand traps, and tiny lakes.

Damon knew Fredo relished a good acting job. He kicked the dirt and swore as well, placing his hands on his hips and shaking his head from side to side. "Son of a bitch, the guys have their own private golf course. That just sucks, man."

Damon couldn't think of anything so he just put his hand to his mouth, while Jason continued to search the horizon.

"You got it on autopilot then?" Damon asked.

"Yup. She'll do a cute little thirty-minute cycle. Then when she's done, she'll beep me, and I'll get her back up into the clouds and bring her back from the direction of town. Unless they've got something special, no one will ever know they've been mapped."

Fredo barked his command. "Everyone spread out and pretend we're looking for parts, okay? Like we think it exploded or something. Pieces. We're looking for pieces."

So while everyone searched, picking up interesting rocks and shell casings, the little bird was busily making them a map of the entire site. Damon was first to find a dead animal: a snake, and the head had been shot off. Coop had switched off the screen but was careful not to cut the power. He tucked the console in the back of his khakis and went on the search with the other three.

Damon heard the high-pitched beeping alarm of the monitor, which was Coop's cue to turn it back on, tap it again, even hold it up to his ear like he was listening for signs of life, then abruptly turn facing town, and shield his eyes as the drone made a perfect landing in front of him but coming from the opposite direction than the villa they were monitoring.

He unclipped the wing element, folded it in half on tiny hinges, and stored it, the body and other peripheral items in his backpack. Before zipping the bag up, Damon noticed he'd hit an arrow button on his monitor, the faint acknowledgement of something accepted, and then slid the monitor into a padded sleeve.

The four of them walked toward town. It was hard to tell where the road was at first, but slowly a worn section of red clay dirt appeared, along with a small curb. The newly formed road T-boned into a busier roadway that wove back and forth but generally headed toward town.

On the way, Fredo stuck his thumb out along the

two-lane freeway, and a pickup truck bursting at the seams with family members in the four-door cab stopped and allowed them to ride in back with a goat that was tied to a hook mounted to the bed of the truck. It headed toward the Marina.

The ride was less than five minutes, but they exchanged waves and wished the family well. The men traveled the rest of the way on foot, toward the smell of sea water and a particular restaurant that specialized in crab tacos and boasted the largest margaritas in town.

It was their designated rendezvous point.

The restaurant didn't have any front doors, just a metal sliding grate that was pulled across the gaping entryway. Wicker tables and brightly colored chairs dotted throughout the inside of the place, closer to the fans and air conditioners. Outside under grass palapas, it was also very pleasant, and they could watch the population driving and walking past.

Kyle's group was slightly late but eventually arrived.

He sat close to Coop. "They're working on the upload you sent them. Said the pictures were excellent."

Coop patted his backpack. "She does real good work."

"Did you learn anything?" Damon asked his LPO.

"We have a minor wrinkle in that General Cortez is in residence at the present time. He didn't see us, but, well, I don't have Kelly yet to work something out with her people. If he cooperates, I think the price will go up from before."

Damon had been told that, on one mission, the general was awarded a bright cherry red Tesla at the border for his troubles in helping them with a mission. But the verbal promise Kyle made to him was also that one of his guys would marry the general's daughter. Luckily none of the bachelors from that trip were with them this time, but Kyle explained that they were to give him a wide berth.

"I'm not sure how he figures in here, but with the level of smuggling rising astronomically, it's no accident he's here, which means his prices are inflated should we need his protection."

"I've never met him," said Damon.

"He's hard to forget, even without his red Tesla," said T.J. "He likes his medals."

Kyle turned toward him. "He's got a house just over the border, and that's where the Tesla is stored. He also happens to have several beautiful daughters, and they would have to be to get any takers. I mean, who wants him for a father-in-law?"

"I feel sorry for the girls. They didn't ask to be born into that family," said Danny.

"You think he might know about Kelly and Ridgeway? Can that be exploited any way?" asked Tucker.

"That's a good question, and I don't have an answer right now. Problem is, even though you two are native speakers, we don't know who the movers in town are. A lot could have happened since we were here last, so who knows what side Cortez is on." Kyle stood up to slip into the head.

Coop asked Trace and Tucker, "Was he alone or with his men?"

"He was with a handful of non-uniforms. Fairly clean-cut. Could be military or undercover, maybe cops, maybe government types. He's got an angle somewhere," answered Tucker. "He was definitely doing business."

"I think, if we run into him, we say it was intentional, flatter him a bit. Let him know there's something for him in it if he helps get her out alive. Them, I mean," barked Fredo. "You gotta figure people promise things all the time. We've never not paid him."

"Only when none of us came back to marry his daughter," said Armando coolly. He was wearing his shades, even though the palapas threw everything into near darkness. It was sort of his signature, part of his uniform.

Pitchers of beer and margaritas instantly appeared just as Kyle was returning from the rest room.

"Your little bird did good, Coop. The commander is pleased."

A group of very drunk American tourists, mostly college-aged men, passed by, attracting attention. "Dumb farts," he mumbled under his breath.

"Oh, come on, football jock like you—you never came down here for a good time, spring break and everything?" Fredo said.

"What you sayin', Fredo? They're probably not much older than I am. And as for college, well, take a gander. I don't think anyone here except Kyle ever went to college."

Danny Begay raised his hand. "Semester at the J.C. and I even managed to pull off a one-point-oh G.P.A. before I got expelled."

"See?" Damon said, defiantly.

"I got an AA degree in nutrition and weight training," said Tucker.

"Shrek, you're the highest educated one of us all then!" said Kyle, hand-slapping him a five.

"I took a cultural anthropology class at University of Hawaii just so my grandma would stop yelling at me. The teacher was right off a sailboat from Tahiti, and she wanted to surf, so I taught her how—for extra credit," Jason shrugged, pretending to be embarrassed.

"I rest my case, sir," Damon bowed onto the table toward Fredo.

The L.A. native wasn't pleased. His eyes were getting rheumy. Both he and Armando had consumed almost one entire pitcher of margaritas by themselves. Damon could see something was eating away at Fredo, and he thought perhaps he'd scratched something that was still bleeding, an old wound.

He was going to say something back, but Coop kicked him under the table. Then he asked Fredo if he'd been able to pick up any stray conversations, anything of interest. Kyle added his approval.

Fredo pressed his shoulders back, cracking his neck, then leaned forward, balancing his head on the tripod of his clasped hands over his elbows.

"There's a lot of stuff in the air. Lots of tourists, people who are not paying or tipping well, have little money, but sort of flaunt themselves at the local population, you know? They haggle and bargain, not because they need to, but just for the fun of depriving someone of money to feed their families."

Damon wondered if that was the source of the older SEAL's frustrations. He suspected it was more than that.

Armando added, "I've been hearing complaints too. Like people handing servers tips, peanut change, really, and smiling, expecting them to be so grateful. A lot of people here because it's a cheap place to go. There's a lack of respect. I've never seen it that way before."

"Yeah, and they're getting in the way. The locals are

trying to make sure the tourists have a good time, and they're worried. We all know where the big money is. I think if the cartels had it their way, they'd send all the tourists away so they wouldn't have to worry about upsetting their uncle to the north," said Fredo. He gave a quick look at Damon but didn't hold eye contact. "Tension. I feel tension, Coop."

"Maybe that's why the massacres and holdups of the vacationers," added Kyle. "Maybe they're trying to discourage or depress tourism a little bit."

"But this is the bread and butter for the unconnect-ed people," began Armando. "It's just that now, it's literally pennies compared to what they can make in the trafficking trade. I think some of them resent it."

"Well, it is their country," added Damon. "I can see how they'd feel disrespected because many tourists don't understand the culture or they have a fictional concept of it. Something they've seen on TV."

"It's more than that, Damon," Fredo said softly. His tone was lightening, indicating to Damon he'd been working on his attitude, keeping some of his emotions in check. "It's really more like they don't feel they need our dollars anymore. Or not these dollars. They're earning hundreds of times more than most the people coming to visit. I don't think they like hiding it."

"That's dangerous," whispered Kyle. "That's being drunk with power."

"Nobody treated them benevolently. Why should they return the favor?" Armando said behind his shades. The comment made Damon shudder inside.

The balance of power was indeed changing. It was dangerous, unpredictable, and not likely to do anything but get worse over the coming months. Damon could see it wouldn't end well.

"All the more reason to get our people out now, because time is not on our side," he added.

"Most definitely," Fredo said, nodding his head solemnly. "Most definitely."

CHAPTER 12

CARLTON GREEN CALLED Martel before eight o'clock.

"The attorney for the Gibbs, a Mr. Manny Risso, wants a meeting in my office this morning at ten. Can you make it?"

"Sure," she said. There wasn't any choice in the matter. "This is just for the attorneys, right? The Gibbs won't be present?"

"Yes. He's going to be meeting with me afterward. He thought it would be best to informally meet with you before he files anything."

"Who is he considering suing, or do you know?" she asked him, beginning to have her first annoyance of the day. She knew it was going to be tough. Part of her resented it.

"Potentially against you and/or the school district."

Martel read between the lines that Green was jockeying for position to be excluded from the proceedings.

Gran Karmody had been right about her administrator. She wanted to ask him why he wasn't named but decided to drop it for now. But she had to tell him about Karmody.

"Mr. Green, I'm going to be bringing in my attorney."

"Uh, well, this is informal, really. Nothing has been filed as of yet. He reassured me he was fact-finding."

"Then I definitely want my attorney there, since he'll be asking me questions, Mr. Green. You know that's the best way to do this. The union would want it that way too."

"You have an attorney from the union already? That's kinda fast. They usually—"

"No, I haven't heard back from them. This gentleman will represent me and only me. I assume the school district will use their counsel."

"Well, if it comes to that. Don't you think that gives off a whiff of some wrongdoing here?" he asked. "If you just talked to him, maybe nothing further will happen. We certainly don't want to escalate things."

Martel wanted to give him a smart retort but knew it wasn't wise. "I don't think I did anything wrong. I was acting in the child's best interest, which indirectly was for the benefit of the parents as well. But I'll go over all that this morning. Let me get hold of my guy so he can be there on time."

"Suit yourself."

"Can I ask you why you won't be in the meeting?"

"We've managed to talk some, and he said he didn't think it was necessary."

"Okay. That's fine. I have no objection to that." She hesitated to bring up her concern about class this morning, even though she'd already decided to ready herself for it just in case.

"I can still go in. I mean, I'm prepared to teach this morning. I'll just need coverage for the meeting, if you can arrange that. But no need for a sub—"

"Already been arranged, Martel. Mr. Risso thought it would be a good defusing type of action, cooling down everyone's tempers."

So you're still setting me up.

Martel was feeling a little better about leaving in June.

Her next action was to call her attorney, who said he'd be there for sure, but wasn't sure about the woman he was referring to the case. "I want you waiting for me outside the school, so I don't have to hunt down the offices."

"No problem."

"I want you to dress up a bit, a little nicer than you normally go into school."

"Funny, I had thought to do the same."

"Olivia Noriega is a very bright shining star from

Sarasota. I met her as a young law student when the class was working on a project pro bono."

"Okay. Has she worked on cases like mine?"

"I believe so."

"What was the project?" she asked.

"It concerned a woman who had been wrongly charged with child abuse and then convicted and had been separated from her family of five children while serving ten years. I helped them draw up and file petitions on the woman's behalf. They were successful because of how doggedly she took on this case. I'm going to see to it that she either gets appointed a judge or runs for public office. She's that good. I talked to her last night after you and I talked, and she's very interested. Now, don't get your hopes up about today, but she'll definitely help out."

"I look forward to meeting her."

"Who did you say the other attorney is?"

"Oh, let me think. Mr. Green told me it was Manny Risso. I don't know anything about him. Of course, I can count on one hand the number of attorneys I actually know."

"Manny Rizzo. That's good. That's really good. I'm sure Olivia will be pleased."

"Is he tough? My administrator says this is to be informal, that he'll have some questions for me, things that might affect whether or not he actually does file a lawsuit."

Gran Karmody laughed into the phone. "Sure. He wants to take the temperature of his case and get a hint of how he should write it up. As far as if he's good, I've never opposed him before, but I understand he can be quite charming. And he has a nice smile, according to that billboard in the Publix parking lot."

"Don't forget the bench."

"Yup, that too."

"So you aren't worried."

"Well, he just tried to pull off something very obvious, and we're going to stop that. He tried to get in there and interview you without representation, and he tried to get your administrator, who is scared to get involved, to grease the skids for him. It's a sleazy maneuver, and he'd never try it if he knew he was up against somebody good, so he's already made his first mistake—he's underestimated you, us, the situation. But don't worry, he'll quickly adjust."

"Okay, then. I'll see you at ten. Do I bring anything?"

"Just dress for success, like it was a big job interview. Look as perfect as you can be, which shouldn't be hard. And don't do a lot of talking. I'm going to step on your foot if you do too much of that. Save it for the judge, if it goes that far."

It was going to be a hot February day, not unusual

for Florida, but she changed her mind on what she was going to wear. She took off the slate blue suit she had put on over her white long-sleeved blouse with the self-tie at her neck and put on a light blue seersucker suit over a short-sleeved silk blouse with a smooth neckline. She put on her mother's pearls, twisted her hair up to keep her neck cool, and felt much more comfortable.

Using the restroom before she left, she saw a light pinkish bleed on the toilet tissue and figured her period would be starting soon. She'd been slightly concerned that her period was late but chalked it up to the stress of her California visit. Now she could relax a bit with one less thing to worry about.

It never ceased to amuse her that, while she was readying herself for a big meeting, the rest of the people in the Sunset Beach area were on vacation. It was one of the things she loved about the Florida Gulf Coast, a much-needed reminder, especially this morning, about the fact that the whole rest of the world was operating at a different vibration. The pilgrimage to the white sand and surf had begun and would continue until the bright sunsets. She was going to have to find that same routine back in San Diego, because it was soothing, healing, and it kept her sane.

She saw parents with young children crossing Gulf Boulevard, wearing clothing they wouldn't be caught dead in elsewhere. Men normally dressed in business attire here could wear loud flamingo prints and straw hats, sunglasses, and flip flops, their arms laden with towels and coolers or pulling wagons with big wheels. The golf cart rental business was booming, since it was peak season. In this community, they were an adult form of four and six-seater bumper cars. People decorated them with lights, particularly when celebrating special events like Halloween, weddings, and bachelor parties. And unlike the Miami area, this part of the Florida Gulf Coast was a senior citizen paradise, a mini-Disneyland with endless warm days and shockingly beautiful sunsets.

It felt odd heading off to her school anticipating being served with a lawsuit.

She'd have to remember not to take things too seriously—at least not until she had to.

Gran Karmody was waiting for her in the parking lot, dressed in his signature white linen suit and string tie. Next to him stood a petite Latin woman with jet-black slightly wavy hair she wore back in a clip. She wore a stylish navy-blue suit and light-yellow shirt underneath with pumps that gave her a couple of inches extra height. Next to Mr. Karmody, she almost resembled some of the girls in her class. If Ainsley stood next to her, she'd tower over the woman.

Karmody was a little slow with the introductions,

so she extended her hand, cutting him off.

"Olivia Noriega, nice to meet you." Her handshake was firm and all business. Her smile was genuine.

"Martel Long. Thank you for coming on such short notice." She asked, "Anything you need from me? We have about five minutes."

"Gran has filled me in. Only thing I want you to do is not to answer anything unless we say it's okay to do so. But don't make it obvious. Make it natural. And don't be nervous, no matter what you hear, okay?" the attractive attorney said.

"I always say walk in a couple of minutes early and catch him off guard a bit. Attorneys are always late."

"Good idea," said Olivia. "Do you have any questions, Miss Long?"

"Oh, please call me Martel."

"Fine. If you need to talk to us in private, you ask for that. Or ask to use the restroom, and I'll go with you, so don't be concerned if that happens."

"I pee a lot when I get nervous. It will probably happen."

"Perfectly natural," she said and gave Martel a wide, generous smile.

"Show the way, little lady," said Mr. Karmody.

Martel walked ahead of them, passing classrooms in session. She could hear the lessons being taught and the students answering, and she saw hands go up. She felt so much more comfortable in class. That was her environment, not the administrator's office.

They walked into the Attendance Office, and she greeted the school secretary seated behind the long counter. "Good morning, Shirley. We're here to meet in Mr. Green's office."

"Oh yes, dear. They're in there now." She leaned forward. "I think you can go in," she whispered, pushing her purple glasses back into her nose.

Martel turned left, crossing a series of teacher boxes, some worktables for students who had to spend study time in the administrator's office or who waited for parents to pick them up, the school nurse's office, on to the closed door of Mr. Green's office. She knocked.

Green was sweating already, reminding Martel that the office had always had trouble with the air conditioning system. His eyes darted behind her, studying the two attorney she'd brought, and then he focused back on Martel. "Manny's all ready for you." And then to the attorneys, he extended his hand, "I'm Carlton Green, the school administrator. Thanks for coming."

Gran Karmody was the first to speak. "Mr. Green, you have yourself a fine little school here. Nice and clean, I can see why my client loves teaching here."

Martel noted that Mr. Karmody was going to allow the misconception he was just a good old boy, a country lawyer in over his head. Green made a slight grunt, passing right by him and shaking Olivia Noriega's hand.

"Nice to meet you, Mr. Green. I'm Olivia Noriega."

"You're not from around here, are you?" Green asked.

"Not far. My office is in Sarasota."

Manny Risso, recognizable by his pencil-thin moustache from the famous billboard, was not much taller than Ms. Noriega, which surprised Martel. He appeared in the doorway and immediately lit up when he saw her.

"Olivia! Why, it's been too long."

Administrator Green appeared ill at ease and quickly retreated into one of the other little offices while the two attorneys briefly caught up.

"Manny and I were classmates in law school," she said to Martel, following it up with a pert smile.

"Well, this is most excellent. Most excellent. Great to be working with true professionals and old friends. Why that just makes it even better." He turned his back and entered Green's office. Martel and Olivia shared a look between them until Ms. Noriega rolled her eyes.

"After you, ladies," Mr. Karmody said.

Manny Risso sat in Carlton Green's chair, in front of the plaques he'd earned as Teacher of the Year and then Administrator of the Year. Other service club awards and pictures of him with students at science fairs and two Halloween carnivals, as well as a Rowdies game with several of the parents, served as a backdrop.

Except that Manny looked ridiculous sitting there. The chair was too low, and the desk came up mid chest such that he looked like a sixth grader sitting at his dad's desk. He had a yellow notepad already filled with a couple of pages of notes, folded back on itself. He spoke to Martel first.

"I think Carlton explained what we're doing here, Miss Long. This is just an informal meeting to go over some of the allegations—opinions, if you will—so we have a basis and context on which to start."

Before he could utter another word, Olivia inserted herself.

"Start what?"

Risso sat up straight, beginning to realize how undersized he was sitting at the large desk of a very large man. "Well, to check out the facts."

"Why don't you tell Gran and I what the facts are, as you see it, first. And then we'll respond."

"Well, obviously it's early, and we're still gathering the details. I thought Miss Long could fill—"

"We'd like to know what was communicated to you. You've had some discussions with Mr. Green, but you haven't communicated anything to our client. So why don't you fill us in?" she said, smiling.

Risso squirmed under the three sets of eyes on him, and Martel could see he hadn't quite prepared to do most of the talking but now was going to have to.

"Okay, we can start there. But I would like to get Miss Long's side of the story, if you don't mind."

Olivia Noriega re-crossed her legs and leaned forward, tapping a red polished forefinger on the edge of the dark oak desk. "Let me be blunt, if I may, Mr. Risso. We aren't here talking about suing your clients. Our only interest is two-fold. First, we'd like to see the young girl in question…" She turned to Martel.

"Cora Gibbs."

"We'd like to see Cora Gibbs and her home evaluated by the Pinellas County Sheriff. The reason is obvious. If there is some type of abuse going on, whether it's in the classroom or the home or elsewhere, we'd like to see her evaluated by a professional. We'd like the parents on the record in the evaluation. And second, after you give us your take on the whole situation from your client's standpoint, if our client wishes to and we advise it, she'll answer questions." She tapped the desk several more times. "But not until then."

She sat back in her chair, and, as an afterthought, plastered a smile on her face.

Risso's expression reflected the sudden realization he was headed straight toward a powerful locomotive, and he was driving a Volkswagen Beetle.

CHAPTER 13

KYLE HAD COORDINATED with the commander's team that they'd do a visual with their NVRs. They were also to take the other drone with the infrared camera and do a direct upload to Coronado so the Headshed could see in real time what they were up against. It wasn't to be a raid, per se. In fact, they were to get in and out without anyone being detected, unless conditions were stellar and they could remove both the hostages safely at the same time.

He told them State was negotiating with the Mexican government, but it was not being fruitful. Through diplomatic channels, they'd been told that the government officially had no ties to the group that took the two Americans and said they were trying to establish communication. But the days were ticking along. Two days were already too long.

Everyone agreed.

This was all standard, required channels since

Ridgeway and Kelly were both federal employees, and Ridgeway's rank was nearly that of an ambassador. Only difference was that he couldn't order in troops or call an air strike independent of the dudes at Coronado.

They were sitting in their huge common area table back at the housing project, just after the domestics and cooks had left for the day. Damon thought the food was delicious, especially the artfully arranged fruit platters they munched on all day and well into the evening.

He was waiting for a chance to call Martel again. His first message went direct to voicemail.

"I don't get it, Kyle. How come there's no random demand, no contact with anyone in Baja," said T.J. "It's not like there will be some prisoner exchange."

"It's because they want something else," a heavily-accented voice boomed from the direction of the front door.

Damon turned around and saw Sven Tolar completely blocking the entrance. A former FSB, Norwegian Special Forces operator, Sven had stayed behind to meet with a small commando team Kelly's father-in-law had been organizing to work like a NGO, providing backup and intelligence for the Navy. He was to accompany Team 3 when they were tasked with a mission, but with Kelly's capture, he dropped everything and came as fast as he could on his own.

He was Kelly's fiancé.

"Was wondering if you'd show up," mumbled Tucker as he came over to give Tolar a brief hug and fist bump.

Tolar dropped his duty bag and joined them at the table, reviewing maps Kyle had spread out. "My theory is that they don't want to negotiate with the Americans. They can make more money negotiating with the other cartel who was here before. They follow a former Marine, Carlos Gutierrez, who comes from a wealthy family in Monterey and hung for a time with Delta Group as a special terrorist group search and destroy unit. Except he turned on Uncle Sam, started lining his pockets with gold and equipment, recruited half his team, and went AWOL."

"He's part of the California Surf Club, then," said Damon.

"That's them. I see you're focused on the villa," he said, pointing to it on the map. "Carlos knows the State Department isn't going to want to negotiate with him, because of the double cross he played on Uncle Sam. I think he's thinking he could get more by negotiations with the old Cortez brothers."

"The general?" said Kyle.

"Cousins. Same family. The general is a minor player, but he does have the ear of the President of

Mexico, and he controls a sizeable militia, all state-owned but used to enhance the family's assets."

"And what value are they to Cortez?"

"Why, they save the U.S. Special Agents and curry favor with Washington D.C. That means more—like foreign aid, cooperation in Mexico's economic development plan, etc."

"And forfeit their holdings in Baja," said Trace.

"It's a small price to pay. They will get protection here. The turf war stops, and everyone goes back to their corners."

"It's kinda brilliant, if you think about it," said Kyle. "The Surf Club gets the girls and drugs between Baja and the US without having to watch their backs. They hand the Cortez group something they want, a direct line to elements in our government who might want peace and safety for its citizens on vacation. Not to mention lucrative contracts to partner and build more hotels all over the resort areas, not just Baja."

"Exactly," beamed Sven.

"Have you or anyone had any contact with either of them?" Kyle asked.

"Ridgeways has been disabled or temporarily removed," said Sven. "Not sure what that means."

Damon could see the burden of Kelly's kidnapping weighed heavy on him.

"Tonight, we're going for a look-see. I'm assuming

you'll want to come." Kyle's tone was flat, his eyes downcast. There wasn't much anyone could say to make Sven feel better. Damon knew he just wanted to see with his own eyes she was okay.

"You sure we can't pull off an extraction?" Sven pleaded. "These things are fluid. They might make a deal, and then she'd be shipped out. I know the bosses will do everything they can to keep her alive, but the rank and file?" He shook his head. "They can be careless. And some of them don't have much of a moral code, if you know what I mean."

"We'll get her," said T.J., placing a hand on his shoulder. "She's one of us. She's kept a bunch of us alive more than once. Now, your sorry ass, I'm not so sure."

Everyone had a good laugh at that one.

"You go on up and take a shower, Sven. Take the room upstairs on the left, at the end next to mine. Everyone else's paired up, so you'll have the suite closest to the equipment room."

"What did I do? Is it my feet? My snoring?"

"It's your breath, Sven. You fish-eating Norwegians need to brush your teeth more often."

The men started to scatter. Kyle shouted instructions. "Get some rest. We head over there after nightfall, nineteen hundred. On foot."

The collective moan was laced with some heavy

descriptions of sexual activity.

Damon approached Kyle. "I'm going to call Martel before it gets too late. She's gonna ask me how much longer we'll be here. I'm gonna tell her a month. Will that work?"

"Sounds about right."

Damon turned to go, but Kyle called out to him.

"Hey, anything going on between you and Fredo?"

"Not that I know of. I thought I was imagining things there for a bit this afternoon. I thought something might be going on at home."

"Okay, well, keep your distance."

"Why, what has he said?"

"I probably shouldn't have mentioned it. He's got a thing for kids. And, well—"

"I wasn't there, sir, because I didn't know about it." Damon had considered this briefly but didn't figure it was germane.

"Just leave him alone and don't engage. He'll toughen up."

"Toughen up? What does *he* have to toughen up about? He's got more kids than—"

"Watch it, Damon. Don't go comparing yourself to others, especially on this team. It's a dangerous occupation. If they feel you, as a newbie, need to be put down, they won't even think twice about it. He's senior around here, trying to make it to twenty like all the rest of the old guys here. You got four years on your first hitch. You're still in diapers, Damon, and don't forget it."

Damon realized he'd just been dressed down. It happened so fast it was over before he knew what was happening. He'd heard the stories about how there were highs and lows of any SEAL team. Some teams never gelled, like Team 4 in Virginia where Andy had gone. They'd lost guys they shouldn't have, including some on training exercises, which was a total waste. But they trained with everything live and real, so it happened.

Team 3 had been spared their share of problems, and that was mainly due to the solid core of the "old guys," as Kyle said it, who held everyone in check and who trained the tadpoles. They didn't have any super-stars or whiners. They had lots of specialists in different fields, and there was a clear hierarchy of who was senior and who was learning. Kyle let them do that, as a good LPO should. Some were more heavy-handed, and if they lacked confidence, things could erupt and fracture or that glue would never form.

Damon hoped it was a temporary lull that just hap-pened sometimes. He'd heard his grandparents talk about being married for sixty years, and even they had good years and bad years, they said. The team was a family, after all. From year to year, not everyone loved everyone the same.

Fuck it.

Now he was starting to question himself. He'd ruled out Fredo's mocking and correction as just that time of the month, but maybe he hadn't been paying attention to things. Now it was going to dog him, too.

It was time to do something else. He ran up the stairs and heard Jason in the shower. He decided to call her first, so he'd have privacy, and then take his shower and hit the bed.

"Damon, oh, I can't believe it. I so needed to hear your voice tonight."

"Everything okay?"

"Well, I don't want to talk about it, actually. You shouldn't have to burden yourself with it. I'm getting some help. I'm not feeling all alone, so no need to worry."

He did hear the wiggle in her voice, that part that came from the back of her throat just before she started to cry.

"Better tell me now, Martel. Otherwise, I'm going to worry about it all night long."

"Don't be silly. It isn't anything I can't handle."

Damon felt the pressure of not having a lot of time to spend on the phone. Calls were supposed to be short. Otherwise, it set up a pattern in the cell towers and created curiosity, if anyone was listening. Long calls were always frowned upon anyway, because there was a lot of friction created between the older guys, who never had cell phones or facetime chats from home, and all the new "spoiled" SEALs who had all this fantastic equipment. They could talk to their naked wives and speak to their kids so that, when they got home, they'd recognize them. It had been that bad. A lot of marriages were lost due to lack of communication. So it did make some angry, resentful.

"Tell me." He wanted to swear for emphasis.

"I think I told you I was having a parent-teacher conference because of some behavior I'd seen at school. I told you that, right?"

"Yeah, and you told me you weren't supposed to talk to me about it, so I quit asking. And you said it went well."

"It did. Until—"

"Until what?"

"Until they got a lawyer involved. A personal injury lawyer. And they're doing this dance about me not keeping her safe at school. *I'm* the one who demanded the conference. And I'm required to report things that I see, based on my admittedly limited experience, that don't look normal. It's not just what the school wants or I want. It's the law. I could have just let Child Services go over there unannounced or the sheriff, but I sat them down to explain what I'd seen and what was going to happen. I also asked them to take the advice of the professionals and get Cora some counseling, maybe the whole family."

"What did the sheriff say? Or am I not supposed to ask that question?"

"I can't get too much into the details, but this now is going to concern me, us, so I sort of feel obligated to tell you more than I could before."

"Okay. Look, maybe I should call you back tomorrow."

"You can do that."

Martel's voice faded, sounding like one of her students.

"Sweetheart, whatever it is, I can't imagine it can't be worked out. Besides, they love you there. That school is going to bend over backwards to protect you. There's no way they'd allow you to have to do battle with these parents and their asshole attorney all by yourself. Once they see that, they'll back off and go after someone else. An easier target. Someone who has something to hide. A secret past."

He heard silence on the other end of the phone.

CHAPTER 14

I T WAS LATE, but Martel didn't want to sit around the house tonight, especially alone. Her best friend, Kaitlyn, was nearing her seventh month and would be getting a sub for the remainder of the school year very soon. She had forgotten to tell her the reason for Martel's missing office hours and the sub.

But it was nearly nine o'clock, and Kaitlyn had told her that she often went to bed early these days because she was so big. She could call Aimee Carr, but that felt like she was going outside the school chain of command and might be a little sticky.

So it was Kaitlyn she called.

"Hey, kiddo. I was wondering if you'd gotten back. How was it? Did you get to meet her?"

"I did. She's beautiful, Kate. Big blue eyes just like Damon's. Has his build. She looks like a snickerdoodle with all the little brown freckles over the bridge of her nose and upper cheeks."

"Said by a true mother. Even ugly babies have fans."

They both laughed.

"So how was she to talk to?"

"Well, I think it's a lot to take in all at once. She was a little angry. There was some resentment there I didn't expect. Of course, that could be just my lack of experience. There are a couple of guys on Team 3 who were adopted, and Damon has told me some stories, but I think it's different for a girl and a guy. Or maybe I'm just making excuses."

"Sounds perfectly normal to me. I know I would be very sensitive to it. All these grownups making decisions that affected my life. Thank goodness the adoptive parents are nice."

"They're perfect. She's just like her adoptive dad, and most people they don't bother to tell because she looks and acts just like a clone of him. They're very close. So, yes, I made a lot of poor choices in getting pregnant in the first place but placing her with these people was a good choice. One of the best ones I've ever made."

"I'm glad to hear it."

Kaitlyn must have figured she had something on her mind because she let Martel speak next. That was one of the things Martel enjoyed so much about their friendship. They didn't push, pry, or judge.

"I was wondering if I could come over."

"Okay, this sounds serious. Things okay with Damon?"

"Yes," she lied. "He's on deployment right now, and I'm not supposed to say where, but you know what my favorite drink is, so…"

"Indeed. Strawberry margarita. I get it. I thought you said he was going later?"

"This is a temporary duty, an emergency."

"Okay, well, I hope it doesn't interfere with the timing of the wedding."

"It is what it is." Martel wasn't sure it was such a good idea to see her tonight. "You know, on second thought, maybe I should just take a bath, read a book, go to bed, and try to get some sleep. I really didn't sleep much Friday or Saturday nights, nor after I got home last night."

"And maybe that's why you think you need to have a talk. You could be just tired, Martel."

"You're probably right."

"They do know you're leaving at the end of the year."

"Yes. Mr. Green knows. I haven't said much to the other staff or teachers. Why?"

"Well, I wasn't sure. This morning, Green asked me if there had been anything bothering you, like, why did you fly to San Diego for just a couple of days and then fly all the way back. He wondered what the rush was and why you didn't take more time off."

"I don't think he's ever paid attention when I've asked for time off before. But did he ask you anything else or say anything?"

"Well, he said that he didn't think you'd been your easy-going self lately. He wondered if you were having some kind of personal problems."

"Oh dear. What did you say?"

"I knew you'd told him about the wedding, and I figured you'd told him about leaving at the end of the year. But I wasn't sure, so I just said you were anxious to see Damon and go over the wedding plans."

"And you didn't say anything about Ainsley?"

"Oh God, no. I would never do that."

"As far as you know, he doesn't know about her. Are you sure?"

"Oh, I'd remember if I'd told him that. Trust me, I would never talk about that. It's your story, not mine to tell. That would be unforgiveable."

"Okay. Thanks."

"So now you've got my brain going all haywire. How come you wanted to know about what he asked me? Is there some issue about you finishing out the school year?"

"Absolutely not."

"I saw your car today, but you weren't in class or in

the office. Where were you?"

Martel had two choices. If she told Kaitlyn about today's meeting, their phone call would take an hour or more. She might as well go over to their house. If she didn't discuss it, she might not have an easy time falling asleep.

It wasn't hard to make her decision.

"I'll tell you what, let's go to dinner tomorrow night. Maybe catch an early one?"

"Greg's in bed, but I'll check with him and let you know tomorrow at class. Or are you going to class?"

"No, they've got a sub for me. I'm helping with some things for the district, a special project. I'll tell you more about it tomorrow. In the meantime, don't mention it to anybody. And please don't mention Ainsley to anybody, particularly anybody at school, okay?"

"You got it."

"Thanks."

"No problem. But, Martel, I'm genuinely worried about you. We've got the spare bedroom here, or you can stay up and watch TV all night. Don't be alone. Promise me you'll not stew about any of this?"

"I promise. I'll be fine. Thanks so much, Kate. I'll talk to you tomorrow."

It was nearly nine-thirty, and she was meeting Mr. Karmody tomorrow morning for breakfast. She threw one of her mother's quilts over her shoulders and, without changing her clothes, slipped off her pumps and walked barefoot out toward the surf. It was a full moon with a smudgy warm cream-colored glow commanding the whole sky. She could imagine it was a piece of vanilla cotton candy with a nightlight in the middle of it.

The water hadn't caught up to the temperatures of the warm spring air, so it was jarring at first but didn't take long to get used to it. She could barely make out a couple sitting in the sand just far enough from the surf so that they wouldn't get wet. Someone else was walking their dog, which was illegal on this beach, but at this time of night, it wasn't patrolled. At her back, the glowing interiors of the beach houses began to make objects and the waves visible as her eyes adjusted.

She sat in the sand, watching the moon spread its magic over the whole scene.

Leaning forward against her legs, she rested the side of her face on her forearms piled onto her knees and kept that crouching position until she felt the warmth of her body filling up the space inside her quilt bubble. She inhaled the moist cool air and breathed in tandem with the waves.

She hoped she was making the right decision moving back to California. Aimee had convinced Andy to switch to an east coast team, but Martel knew Damon didn't want to do that. He liked Florida, but California was where he felt most comfortable. Andy had grown up on a farm in the central valley and didn't have the same allegiance.

But that wasn't it, she mused. She would be closer to Ainsley. Although at this point in time, she wasn't sure whether she'd be invited back to the Newberg home. Everything was so up in the air. Now her job was perhaps at stake. Certainly, her reputation was. There were so many things coming at her she felt like she was just in a reactive mode all the time. Not a well-planned out execution, like one of her lesson plans. She was the slowest person on the track team, and everyone needed her to hurry up so they wouldn't lose. And she didn't have the speed or the training the others had, so she was desperately trying to catch up.

She missed her mother, who was courage under fire. She'd know what to do and how to handle this overload. Her mother could have run a whole platoon all by herself.

She missed laughing with Phyllis, Kate's mother, who was probably up there dancing in Heaven with the jazz saxophonist—her fantasy love. The lady who told her to go find her daughter, to find that missing piece of her.

While confronting her past, dealing with a challenge in her present, and planning her flawless future, it was the women in her life that she missed. The ladies who bore their disappointments proudly, did the best they could do, and didn't worry about the rest. Martel wished her mother had met Ainsley, but she had a firm hand in Ainsley's life, even though her daughter might never know. It didn't make the gift of her love any less.

"Is this seat taken?" came a familiar male voice next to her. It was Carl Frame, her new neighbor.

"Oh, I was just going to go inside. So, yes, the beach is all yours."

His voice was pleasant. His face was handsome. He smelled good, especially for this hour of the night. Maybe that's what bothered her. He was trying too hard to be someone she really didn't need.

She began to scramble to her feet.

"Wait just a minute. Don't go."

If he came close to touching her, she'd scream. If he actually did touch her, she'd scream louder. "I'm not interested in striking up a conversation, Mr. Frame."

"Call me Carl."

She winced at that, closing one eye. "No, I'm afraid it has to be Mr. Frame. This place is very friendly, but not at nearly ten o'clock at night. It's not appropriate, so I'm leaving."

"You just looked so sad. I spotted you from my living room window, that's all. You looked like you could use some company. I was only trying to help."

"Well, I suppose anyone would look sad at this hour, shivering in the night air on an abandoned beach when they could go inside. But far from being sad, I was thinking. And I can't think when I'm talking, so I'm afraid I must insist that you leave me alone and let me get back to my place."

"Walk you safely there?"

The guy wouldn't quit. That set off the bells and alarms, made the hair at the back of her neck stiffen. The quilt draped around her shoulders would be no defense. She needed a weapon. She inhaled and, as loudly as she could, shouted, "Go away and leave me alone!"

A couple of dogs barked, and two porch lights came on. She was prepared to yell again if she even heard him following her. She ran all the way to her back door, which she'd left open, the last time she would do that, whirled around, and locked it. Then she ran to the front door and locked it as well. She turned off all the lights in the house and peered out her kitchen window to see if he was still out there.

She didn't see anyone on the beach, or her patio. But she did hear a sliding glass door shut and click locked.

She closed every blind and window covering she could find, shut her bedroom door and locked it from within, put the water on in the shower and then undressed, leaving her suit draped over her chair and her underwear where they lay on the bathroom floor. She found a long flannel nightgown that always managed to make her feel cozy, spreading it out on the bed.

The shower was heavenly. Even though she didn't

have time to dry her hair, she still washed it and would deal with the tangles and odd cowlicks in the morning with some hairspray. She applied a facial scrub, then rewashed it with her scented gel face wash, used the lavender shower gel to make her skin squeaky clean, and shed all the negativity of the day. She was baptized in the heavenly lathers and scents, washing away all her sins and becoming fresh and new, just like the Easter Sunday when she'd gotten dunked and joined the church. This was the reset to her life she needed right now.

She loved the towel warmers the owner had installed, and tonight, as she wrapped and patted herself, they were nearly orgasmic. It felt good to stretch down and touch her toes, drying her lower legs, her thighs, and finally her upper thighs between her legs.

The towel came back light pink, one small stain that was unmistakable. Her belly didn't feel like it was going to erupt and release the monthly blood and fluid it automatically stored each month.

She checked her underwear on the floor, and it, too, had a thin band of pink, a small discharge of blood. Very watered-down blood. Spotting, really.

Just like she'd had with Ainsley when she first got pregnant.

CHAPTER 15

DAMON WASN'T THE only one who was annoyed at the five-mile run and the foothill hike. He just couldn't see expending that much energy when they could have had the vans drop them off much closer.

The explanation that Kyle didn't want the drivers to know what they were investigating just didn't sound reasonable enough for all the effort it was going to take. He thought, perhaps, they would have been better off conserving their strength. It wasn't that it was a five-mile run. It was a five-mile run near the hottest part of the afternoon, in more than eighty-degree weather. He saw huge clouds billowing up from the other side of the little mountain range to their East and prayed for rain, as a matter of fact.

Each of them brought a backpack, and instead of their regulation black duty bags, they'd been instructed to bring something a non-SEAL would use. Several guys used their daughters', covered with unicorns and pink rabbits. Kyle had borrowed Brandon's Captain America backpack, which was somehow fitting.

They ended their run toward the beach side then traveled through scrub brush, stunted desert trees, and cacti until they found a deep but narrow river that flowed out to sea. It came from up in the foothills and then meandered past the villa. If they followed along the banks, it would leave fewer footprints, even if their run had attracted attention. It wouldn't be of use now, but on the return trip, a little boat would do nicely, and they could just float back to the beach. He wondered if Kyle had considered using another method.

He stumbled several times, scraped his ankle on the sharp outcroppings, and kicked himself for not wearing socks he could pull up and protect his lower legs.

And there were bugs and poison cactus needles to avoid.

The base of the foothill the villa stood on was very gnarled and rocky, with cracks and cervices everywhere, as if it had been some ancient lava flow. Kyle pondered which way to approach the outcropping when Armando found a cave, which faced South, so the inside was well lit but cool. A smelly pool of green water had seeped in, no doubt remnants of a winter hurricane, as was prone in this region. During one such storm, one of these tributaries grew so fast that it overflowed and wiped out the first floors of several older hotels downtown as it traveled out to sea and disappeared. The town was still finding old mattresses, bedframes, and luggage the Sea of Cortez was trying to return. He'd seen a picture of an abandoned Coke machine and a half dozen refrigerators. It had also swept through a local truck dealership, and for weeks afterward, Ford pickups were finding themselves marooned on the beautiful beach, delighting all the tourist children.

Like everything else about Mexico, Damon always found something so totally unexpected and juxtaposed to something else that didn't belong there. He just prepared himself for the bizarre and macabre. There was a level of violence that he could almost smell, and it infected everything.

Maybe that's what I'm picking up. Fredo had been raised in East L.A. in a very tough, gang-infested neighborhood even back then. His father was murdered, and his mother sent him to join the Navy to get him out of L.A. He'd been running on the edges of beginning to get into trouble. The Navy completed the job his parents could no longer do. Damon knew Fredo was grateful for the chance to prove himself, finding a true family in the Brotherhood, and often spoke of it. Especially when someone's past came up. He was the conscience of the group, the one to remind everyone that their bond wasn't just lip service. It was everything.

But there was something dangerous going on with him this trip, perhaps harkening back to his Latino roots, and Damon was going to take Kyle's advice and steer clear of him.

In the cave, Kyle laid out a map he'd brought with him, a rough sketch of the surveillance footage sent back from Coronado on Coop's little bird.

"We're going to do some eyes-on surveillance of the villa since the likelihood is that we'll only have one shot at it. If it's too risky, we're to pull back. At the present time, there is no deal made on transferring the hostages out to someone else," Kyle began.

Damon and the others gathered around the sketches placed on a sticky page.

"She's here, we think, or at least that was the last sighting. Just like before, the last known signal from Ridgeway was from here. And it does look like a shipping container, which would explain the poor signal."

"You want us to scope out some good sniper locations if we need it later?" asked Armando.

"Exactly. You and Danny find four vantage points, two for each of you. Then you decide which ones will work, depending on what we find when we come back."

"Roger that," said Danny.

"Fredo, I want you and Damon to locate where and how you'll set up the charges."

Damon peered at Kyle, and then saw his smirk. He had decided to *force* them together, after giving him advice against it. He was about to object when he saw Kyle's slight shake of his head, so he shut up.

"You want massive or super massive?" Fredo asked.

"Whatever it is, I want you to blow a hole in the front gate big enough to get that water truck through and not get it stuck in the debris field."

Damon nodded. "What will they be protecting?" he asked.

Fredo pressed his stubby forefinger onto three other rectangular boxes near Ridgeway's location.

"What about the storeroom? Wouldn't they want to protect the guns and ammo?" he asked.

Cooper shook his head. "No, they'll do that underground, not on top where it's vulnerable to sunlight and surface explosions. They'd keep it cool, probably in a cave. I'm betting there is one here somewhere."

"I agree," said Kyle. "If we get them tasked with putting out the fire, and if they don't see or hear a big army or militia coming for them, they'll be focused on something else. The human cargo is where they make their money. Of course, they'd protect Kelly and Ridgeway too."

"Looks like she's over near the main part of the villa. You think they're actually putting her up in the house?" asked T.J.

Sven spoke up. "I imagine they need her in good shape, under house arrest, but they know she's State and a non-combatant. And if she's been beat up, the leverage they'll have to negotiate goes down."

"Precisely. Which means, Sven, I want you to smuggle in an Invisio to her, so we have ears."

Sven stood tall, putting his hands on his belt. "Well, I guess I could surrender to them, then, get it to her that way."

Several chuckled, but Kyle's expression was stern. "You are of no value to them, Sven. You wouldn't last an hour in there."

"I'll figure something."

"I want everyone looking at everything, anything we can use to our advantage. Tucker, Trace, and Jason, I want pictures if you can of what's in those squares. How many, ages, sex, how they're guarded. Coop, you be their cover, but you signal the shooters here if anybody gets into trouble. If you have to overtake anyone, make it quiet and very quick."

"What if we have to act, I mean, like tonight?" asked Sven. "We can't get back here in time if we have to jog again. We can't transport anyone if we don't have vehicles."

"We got vehicles, here and here. But, Coop, you see

if they're operational."

"Hold on. I'm—"

"No, I'm not asking you to go around and try starting up the trucks, but just see if they're operational or look like they're being used. And then look to see if we can disable any of the ones we don't need, just in case."

"And I'm doing that while I'm watching these three?"

"I'm not gonna lay a hand on the kid," said Fredo. He winked at Damon. It sent a chill down his spine, but inside, he acknowledged the smack talk as a good sign.

"We might as well bury the charges while we're at it, Fredo," Damon thought.

"That's a good idea. Get it set up ahead of time. You're all right, kid."

Damon crossed himself and gave Fredo a bow. He got a finger for his troubles.

"So you want me to, what, clean my Sig?" T.J. asked.

"You're gonna be the runner in case someone needs help. You can back up any of the activities here, and if you have to, you can run radio to the base. Or call an SOS. I'm going to give you the sat phone, so you guard that thing with your life and stay hidden. You and I will be in good contact," answered Kyle.

"Got it. So where will you be?" T.J. asked.

"I'm gonna find that cave. And you older guys who've been down here before, you holler if you see anyone you recognize, hear?"

Everyone nodded. Kyle checked his watch.

"I have thirteen hundred oh five. Fredo, pass out the Invisios. Everyone, check your equipment. Anything you don't need from your packs, leave it here for now. I'm gonna make one call to make sure we're still a go and get a quick update. Oh, Fredo, you got plastic bags for burying those charges?"

"No, didn't bring any. What if I just use the backpack?"

"One of your boys is going to be mighty upset with you."

Damon examined the Hulk pack that obviously had belonged to one of Fredo's twins.

Fredo shrugged. "As long as I come home."

That put everyone into a quiet mood while they checked their specialized pockets, ammo, knives, and gear. Coop passed around a water bottle while Kyle headed to the mouth of the cave and made his call to the admiral.

Damon searched the faces of his team, saw the resolution written there, the focus, people tasked with doing what they were the best at but working together in a pinch. Trace and Tucker were still sweating from the run. Armando and Danny lovingly wiped down their long guns and carefully stored them on their backs. Cooper ate a granola bar. Jason held on to a carved piece of bone that always hung around his neck and whispered prayers to his ancestors. T.J. checked out a picture he kept of his wife and daughters and then stowed it in the zipper pocket over his heart.

Damon said a prayer, sending strength to Martel and whatever she was dealing with. In his mind, she was on the beach, walking, her long hair blowing in the breeze, holding her sandals casually in one hand while her skirts swished as she trekked through the surf. It wouldn't be long before she'd wear that white dress she'd picked out, and then maybe they could start their family, all over again.

And pick up the pieces of the last one.

"We're on. Nothing new, thank God," Kyle said. "Can everyone hear me?"

They nodded.

Kyle handed T.J. the phone. "Let's all be in position in fifteen minutes. We'll check in and then start our tasks."

CHAPTER 16

IT WOULD HAVE been a stretch to guess her mind would be off of the potential lawsuit, her visit with Ainsley, or her soon-to-be husband away doing dangerous things. Those three were pretty big in Martel's world.

But now there was a fourth.

And she wasn't stupid, either. If she was spotting, well, perhaps it would get stronger and then lead to heavy clotting, and so forth. She knew the stories. So, in addition to the possibility that she was pregnant, which she'd already thought about and dismissed previously, there was this strange déjà vu experience of this happening again. That she hadn't been paying attention. No, it wasn't a bit funny that the two of them were so fertile all it took was a few times together and, wham, she'd get pregnant. That conversation would have to be had much into the distance. Right now, it wasn't funny at all.

So how did she feel about this? Had she not learned her lesson? Her pregnancy had consumed the last remaining time she had with her mother before she passed. In fact, it was the reason she was not able to be at her bedside and say good-bye.

She'd altered forever the lives of three other people, not counting herself and Damon. Ainsley's life was arguably better for the adoption. So was the Newberg's life with the fulfillment of a dream of having a child. The full weight of her actions, or lack thereof, came falling down upon her. She was lucky the first time when she was able to find a loving home for her daughter, but Ainsley was right. It had been an after-thought. Did she look hard enough for Damon? Did he care enough about her? And wasn't it true, while she came to profess her love for her darling daughter that, in reality, Ainsley's feelings had been the least she'd cared about. It was all about raising a child by herself or not being sure what Damon would do or the horrible possibility she could have tried to trap Damon into marrying her. It was a choice she didn't want to make. She didn't want to be that kind of a woman.

Maybe I'm worse.

Her meeting exposed how blindsided she was because she hadn't thought about what Ainsley would think. Her goal had been to convince her that she did it out of love.

But wasn't that a lie?

The truth was, she had no right to have Ainsley in her life, and she was asking everyone to give her a pass—the Newbergs, Ainsley, even Damon.

She didn't deserve a pass. She didn't deserve everyone's understanding or their forgiveness, because she hadn't learned her lesson. She'd just perhaps done it again. How stupid and unthinking could she be?

So now what? She envisioned showing up for a trial, pregnant again, not married, and accused of not paying attention to the care of a child in her charge when she was at school. Wasn't this the same thing? Perhaps a light version of the same issue? Wouldn't she deserve any exploitation the opposing attorney might raise? Her last days as a teacher at the school she loved would be marred in shame and disrespect. It didn't matter that she loved Damon and they were engaged. That wasn't the point. It was that the rules, somehow, didn't apply to her. In her attempt to "fix" things, she was still asking for that passing grade when others had played the game in the right order. She was playing dangerous, loose with her morals, even looser with other people's feelings.

The thought that perhaps she was on the edge of a miscarriage didn't make it any better either. That was a convenient, albeit painful, copout.

How did she really feel about being pregnant

again? And if it was so, how would she ever explain it to Damon or Ainsley?

It was hard getting showered, running her hands over her tender nipples, the smoothness of her soft belly, having that baptism of conscience as she anticipated having breakfast with Mr. Karmody. She'd have this little thought in the back of her head, the possibility, perhaps a hope, that new life was forming again, coming her way. And she'd think about this while chatting with Mr. Karmody about her future. The other part of her future.

On her way to the omelet house, she got a call from Kaitlyn.

"When I didn't hear from you, I worried. And when I decided to let you call me, I worried that was the best decision. So I'm calling you now because I'm worried, Martel. Tell me it's not justified."

She found herself laughing a couple notches below hysterically. She wanted to scream out the window, "Bring it all on!" But, of course, she wasn't going to do that. She was like an iceberg, one third above water, two-thirds below. The below was getting deeper and deeper.

"Martel?"

"I'm on my way to meet Gran Karmody over breakfast. If Greg is free, the offer of dinner is still on the table."

"He said he's got work. I think he just wants me to have a night off with my best friend."

"So let's meet early if you can. Five? Fergus Crab Shack?"

"Perfect. And did you sleep well last night?"

"I did. Took a nice, hot shower and fell into bed."

"He's the attorney who handled the meeting with Ainsley?"

"Yes."

"So does this have anything to do with her?"

"No. Nothing to do with Damon, either. It's a school thing. I'll brief you what I can tonight. In the meantime, not a word of this conversation or about Ainsley or what I did last weekend, okay? Please?"

"Of course. Well, until tonight."

"Thanks so much for calling, Kaitlyn."

Mr. Karmody was on the phone, pacing the parking lot when she arrived. He hung up and then greeted her. He still looked fresh in his white linen suit, but today, he had on a light blue shirt. His signature string tie still firmly balanced on his neck like a garotte.

"I've got a table inside," he motioned, directing her past the hostess to a corner by a window where the light was good.

"Olivia won't be joining us this morning. But I'm glad you could come. How are you holding up?"

She knew better than to tell the truth. "I'm fine.

The worst part of these things is that they come out of nowhere, and they take time to work themselves out, don't they?" she said.

"You've got that right. Personalities, expectations, justice, respect. What is one thing to one person isn't to another. It's all a matter of interpretation."

"What did you two talk about after I left?" she asked.

"Olivia is quite confident they won't have much of a case or won't prevail. Unfortunately, that doesn't mean you'll be spared going through a few things, and I wanted to talk to you about this."

"Is this going to ruin my breakfast?"

"I don't think so. But in either case, I'm buying, so if you don't feel like finishing, don't worry."

"I was worried that the two of them had some history."

"I think it should be the Gibbs who should be worried. Olivia is a formidable attorney. He now knows it's not going to be a walk in the park. But before we get into all this, I want to make sure you understand how things are going to work."

"Sure."

He'd been playing with the plastic menu without looking at it, so when the waitress stopped by, he handed it back to her and asked Martel what she wanted. He ordered and then studied his hands folded on the table without making eye contact with Martel.

"You didn't give your permission to discuss your daughter, so I haven't talked about it with Olivia. But I'd like to."

"Sure. I'm fine with it"

"Okay, good. I'm going to run it by her how much we need to delve into it, but if they are looking for a fat settlement rather than a court hearing, her name might come up. I want you to be okay with that."

"No. I'm not okay with it. That's my personal business. It has nothing to do with them."

"I agree, but if they somehow get hold of that information, I want you to be prepared."

"It's not me that has to be prepared. It would be her parents. She's only twelve. I don't see where she would have any involvement at all."

"Newspaper reporters trying to find a juicy angle for their story. I'm sad to say teachers are getting a bum rap these days."

"I'm aware of that. But this is Florida. I doubt they'll hear about it in Palo Alto. Can't we keep them out of it completely?"

"As I think we should. So I'll talk to Olivia, now that I have your permission."

"What else?"

"She agrees with me. Somehow, we have to find out where the sexual abuse is coming from. She agrees with your assessment that her knowledge of sexual things is not natural and some adult is at fault. It's going to be important to help the sheriff find that person."

"Or persons."

"Yes, it could be."

"Will they share their findings? Or are they being kept from doing anything?"

"That's not up to the attorney or to the Gibbs. The law is very clear in the case of child sexual abuse. The child comes first. There are limits to what the law can do, though. But the child is supposed to be protected first and foremost. So they can't stop an investigation forever. They can delay it, and if they get too much in the way, they can be arrested. Not that we want that."

"So, Mr. Karmody, what's your point? I don't understand."

He looked down at his big hands again, chewing on his lower lip and frowning. "We might have to hire a private investigator. We need someone who knows how to dig into court and other records, see if there is anything in the family history that will give some indication of who's at fault."

"Okay."

"It can be expensive."

Martel knew it was coming down to that.

"How much?"

"Five, ten thousand dollars easily. Goes up from

there. The bottom line is that we have to walk the very narrow path of showing Cora has been damaged by some association and, because of that, unwittingly invited the attention at school. That you had no idea to be careful with her or to watch her more closely. You could not be held to a higher standard than a normal other teacher would. In fact, you went out of your way to be transparent, which I think is obvious."

"And if it's not done right, it will backfire. Make enemies out of the parents."

"Or Cora herself. We don't want her embellishing her story, making you more the target. You can see our problem. Unfortunately, resources aren't what they should be, so the sheriff's department isn't known for their skill in this arena."

"Great."

"They have more work than they have people to do the job. Have you ever seen a wrestling match? One of those big events on TV?"

"In passing. It's not my thing."

"Nor mine. But have you ever watched the referee? Now, do you think they ever are in control? I mean, they don't really stop the fight, do they? Most those guys are half the size of the wrestlers, anyway. And some of it is just show. I'm not saying the sheriff's department is like that, but they are more like referees. They gather up all the information for charges to be filed. Someone has to become the target of the investigation. That shouldn't be Cora. It needs to fall on the shoulders of the sicko who can't stop. And it shouldn't be you, either."

Martel nodded her agreement. "So the detective will do some of the legwork for the sheriff and help them build a case, if there is one."

"That's right. And if you think about it, getting some help for that little girl is paramount. We need to get her the support system that will help her heal. We aren't looking to tear the family apart. But it depends on who did what to whom. Get my drift?"

"I do. And I don't think the father is involved."

"Olivia agrees with me on that too. She thinks your hunch about the wife's family would be a good place to start. That is, if you're willing."

"Do I have a choice?"

"Oh, you do. You most definitely do. You could wait until the school gets served with a complaint, naming you as well. By the time things get filed, they become concrete. Sides start forming. It's why Manny wanted to meet with you 'informally,'" he said, using his fingers in the quote marks, "to get enough facts he could use to make a compelling case. It was sleazy, but it was also smart."

"Well, I've been saving for the wedding. I could invest about five thousand dollars in this, if you think it's money well spent. How much more for your fees, for Olivia's fees?"

"I'm not going to charge you. I think you're looking at another five thousand dollars for her, minimum. That's what I'd propose to do, give her a retainer, and let her work with the private detective to see if they can dig up something on that family."

Martel looked at her breakfast and wasn't going to be able to eat a bite. She wasn't sure what had made her sick, but she knew one thing. The catered dinner in a gazebo out at the beach and the rows of rented white chairs became a distant memory. Since it didn't matter much to Damon anyhow, a potluck dinner at Aimee and Andy's house, cases of wine from the Liquor Warehouse, no bridesmaids or groomsmen, and a cake she could probably bake herself was looking pretty good.

Those beautiful, perfect weddings at exotic destinations were for other people who made different choices with their lives. Maybe she'd get to go to Ainsley's wedding someday where she'd have all that.

She could wait that long.

CHAPTER 17

FREDO AND DAMON waited under the shade of a large outcropping of sandstone, populated with desert plants. They were roughly twenty feet from the left side of the enormous solid metal gate that swung open, so they had adjusted their spot to make sure they weren't caught in it. They could hear guards walking the interior perimeter of the plaster walls lined with broken bottles and barbed wire.

Fredo indicated they were in place a whole two minutes early. Danny and others started whispering their checks as well.

Damon nodded toward the wall. "What are they saying?"

"I think they're talking about where they're going to take their group. I guess these must be part of the Coyote brigade."

"Probably do it all. Cross train. They guard, watch over the hostages, and lead the group over the border, you think?"

"Makes sense. They must have hundreds of these guys. You know they busted a team from Romania with affiliation to the Cortez cartel?"

"The ones they're trying to move out?"

Fredo nodded.

"What would they be doing there?"

"Same as here. Picking up people who want to get out, enslaving them to be mules for them and owing them money if they can't pay up front."

"That's sick, man."

Just then, Fredo put a hand to Damon's chest to make him be still. He listened to the conversation.

"Shit, tonight's a big meeting. Someone from Casa Cortez is in town to negotiate."

Damon was completely still, not even moving a muscle so that Fredo could hear everything. Then they heard Kyle's voice.

"I was going to tell you to cut the chatter, but what the hell did you say, Fredo?"

"Someone's coming tonight. Someone big from Cortez."

"Unfortunate," came the whisper back. "Moves up our timeline. This is no longer a fire. This has just turned into a rescue mission. Bone Frogs, you get those containers scoped out. If no one's there, you let me know pronto. I want pictures, body count."

"Roger that," said Tucker.

"Sven?"

"Working on it. Not there yet."

Damon knew Jason was going to give Kyle a piece of his mind when this was all over. He was barely thirty, not a Bone Frog at all.

Fredo unpacked his equipment, laying the blocks of explosive clay a foot apart, like he was organizing a large solitaire game, in two neat rows. He left the plastic covering on the soft bricks but peeled the top layer off, prying it loose with a plastic knife. He asked Damon to cut ten cords about a foot long and fray the ends slightly. With a small plastic-looking drill bit, he made two holes in the top of every block.

"You using it all up?"

"Might as well. I sure as heck don't want to be running across the desert again with this shit."

He got a reprimand again. "Cut the goddamn chatter."

Fredo motioned with fingers to his eyes and pointed to the piano hinges on the outside of the metal gate. He then indicated Damon should do just as he was doing, digging a pit big enough for a backpack to fit and be covered on the other side. He handed him another folding shovel and indicated there was a straight line extending from the hinge to the pit he was digging, showing that it centered on the weakest part of the gate.

Damon carefully waited in the foliage at the side until he was certain no one was coming along the approach and quietly ran across, positioning himself at the other side, then began digging. He was careful not to let the red clay soil, which was extremely dry, form a cloud of dirt that could be seen by anyone with scopes.

They heard Tucker and Trace confirm there were mostly boys housed in very close proximity, wall to wall mattresses. They appeared to be about thirteen to fifteen years of age. Just kids, really. But they were big enough to carry a fairly heavy load.

"They've been issued brand new backpacks with water, food. They've got a shithole around the corner, and one of the kids brought his backpack," said Tucker.

"Girls and boys, younger kids, in the other house. I'm going to check on Ridgeway," Coop whispered."

"Sure would be nice if I could get a tracking device on that backpack," said Fredo.

"Well, why don't you hop the fence and bring it over to me, then," said Tucker.

"Fuck, that's me. Headed your way now, Fredo." T.J. was coming over to pick up and deliver the little needle with the chip inside.

"Too late for this one, but there will be others," said Tucker.

"How did they get inside?" Damon asked Fredo.

"The gate kind of gaps open when you remove the latch. We walked in."

"Too social," whispered Kyle.

Fredo rolled his eyes. Just then, T.J. appeared from the shadows. Fredo stopped connecting the blocks with the cord and removed the pin from his breast pocket. He showed T.J. how to weave it into an inseam so no one would see it. He gave him two more just for good measure.

"Put this on Ridgeway."

T.J. nodded and disappeared as fast as he appeared.

Fredo laid five of the bricks side by side in the unzipped backpack with a piece of Styrofoam as a spacer, the cords in place, then held them all together with a bungee cord with plastic hook ends. With the last brick, he attached the timer, which he could auto turn on. It was set to go off in ten minutes once activated. He motioned with his fingers splayed. Damon had seen him do this several times before during their workups.

Gingerly, Fredo removed a nylon bag from an outer pocket of the pack, unfolded it, and placed the other bricks and spacers in it. He pointed to the other hole and Damon carried the explosives like a tray of tea and cookies to the second hinge. He laid the packs side by side, like he'd seen Fredo do, then strapped them together with the bungee, and made sure all the tops were indeed connected. If one was disconnected, it could throw the timing off or knock the other cords loose, and they could have a one-block dud.

Fredo attached his timer and then placed the bag against a large rock slightly larger than his hand, angling the bag until it was partway leaning against the piano hinge. Damon knew this was to make sure the angle of the blast kicked the hinge loose from the bottom. Due to the weight of the gate, that would be all it took for it to become completely disabled.

He gave Damon a thumbs-up, zipped up the bag, and motioned for him to cover it with soil.

Coop indicated Ridgeway was in poor shape, lying bloody and unconscious. Checking his signs, he reported that, if he didn't make it to a hospital soon, he wasn't going to make it at all.

"Faint pulse. Dehydrated. Two bad wounds on his right thigh. He's not walking. Possibly a fractured foot and ankle. I got the tracer on him. Administering antibiotics, and I hope he doesn't wake up screaming."

"Got you covered, Coop," whispered Danny.

"Charges in placc. Set for ten once activated," added Fredo.

"You guys get out of there," Kyle barked. "Get around to the back so the walls will protect you."

"I got to be twenty feet away, Kyle," said Fredo.

"I got him." Damon grabbed the remote. "Kids

need a dad."

Fredo was visibly touched but didn't interfere with the transfer.

"Damon, you get the hell out once it blows."

Sven's voice came over the com. "Kelly's been drugged but in good shape. Are we doing this tonight?"

"We are. T.J., that was the last piece of the puzzle. Danny and Armando, on your marks?"

Both indicated they were ready.

"So you want me to make the call?" T.J. asked.

"Let's do it and get a SITREP."

They all heard T.J. tell the commander someone from the Cortez cartel was headed over to negotiate.

A few seconds later, they heard all clear. "We are to wait for the new visitor and nightfall. And then it's up to you. They've already got eyes on us. I'll signal them."

"So now we wait," said Kyle. "Anyone want to tell me their plans for Mother's Day?"

Several laughed. Damon stared at the roadway, listening for a vibration. Fredo stuck by his side for now. He removed his Invisio and indicated Damon should do the same.

"You're all right, kid."

"Tell me that when I don't screw up."

"All you gotta do is push the button. How hard can that be?"

"Then you do it."

"I was going to."

They heard the sounds of trucks. They both replaced their earpieces, and Fredo whispered, "We got trucks coming. Danny? Armando?"

"We got one nice, shiny black SUV, heavily armored, followed by another," reported Armando.

Two? He motioned to Fredo.

"Then we got some covered troop carriers. Yo, the gate fellas," Armando warned. "We got four oncoming."

Damon pushed Fredo to the back while he hid in the bushes under the overhang. The sun was beginning to set, but it was still too light out. He was concerned that too much could be seen without the cover of darkness. But, if the former marines were equipped in any way, they'd have IRVs, just like the SEALs did, so it wasn't to their advantage. Main thing was to get the hostages out before they could be taken away.

He thought about what Martel was doing right now. He had intended to recommend they go to Mexico for their honeymoon, but he was nixing that the longer he was here. He would sure look forward to Florida, the sunsets, and the beach. All he had to do was push the button when the signal was given.

The first SUV stopped at the gate. Two drivers in black sunglasses and suits got out, followed by a couple of Dobermans, big black Dobermans. On a whistle command, the Dobermans started sniffing the gate and around the plaster walls. One was on the right, and one was headed straight for him.

"We got a dog tracking Damon," he heard over the Invisio, followed by some pretty hefty swearing.

Damon didn't want to tell them he'd been bitten by a Dobie when he was young and never trusted them. In fact, he didn't like dogs at all, which most of the SEALs thought was odd. This guy meant business as he tracked his scent from the outside of the hinge on the gate to just outside the thicket where he was holed up in.

"Get up on the rock, Damon," whispered Armando.

Damon tried to get his footing but slipped and fell on his belly. The dog abruptly stopped and started barking.

"They're not inside yet. Gates are still closed," Armando updated everyone.

"If you have to, just blow it," said Kyle.

One of the troop carriers unloaded six or seven armed men, who followed behind the dog. The beast was well trained and wasn't going to attack until commanded to do so. His bark was piercing. Damon could hear shouting from inside the gated perimeter as more men came running.

He knew better than to hide the trigger device in

his pants, so he pressed the button and tossed it into the brush.

"We got ten. Nice knowing ya," Damon said. He considered what his future looked like. He was either going to be shot, mauled by a dog, or blown into a thousand pieces by his own hand. The choice wasn't a difficult one. He'd take death by his own hand any day. But those dogs could do a lot of damage to him in ten minutes.

He tossed the Invisio into the brush so he could at least look like he was not part of a team. He'd forgotten to tell them this, but they'd figure it out. They didn't have to hear him screaming his lungs out anyway as the dogs ripped the legs from his torso.

He slowly removed his KA-BAR and knew he could take care of the first dog but not both of them. A lot of men were running toward him now, and it was close, but he was still in the kill zone. In slow motion, the SUV doors opened. Damon said a prayer for that piece of luck. General Cortez was standing right next to the gate, speaking with someone else, and he guessed it was part of the Surf Club, maybe Carlos Guitteriez himself.

He hoped the team didn't come run to his aid, but instead get Kelly and Ridgeway out, hop in a truck, and get the hell out of Dodge.

In slow motion, like it was a rolling thunder, he saw

the larger of the two dogs leap in his direction, the Doberman's body completely covering his, as the snout went for his jugular. Behind him, Damon could barely see the two hinges of the gate explode, sending one side up into the air about twenty feet, and the other slicing across the horizon, taking the top off the first Suburban.

The blast ruined his hearing, leaving him with an electronic buzz that nearly split his head. It must have been disorienting to the dog, too, because he lay very still. Damon sat up and discovered a metal tie bar from the gate's outer surface had given the dog a lethal blow, severing his spinal cord.

Incredibly, that dog had saved his life.

The wholesale bursting body parts spurting blood and guts all over the ground and chaos that erupted in complete radio silence was surreal. And where the general had been, all that was left were his two well-polished boots, still standing as if he was in a salute, fragments of the general's lower legs protruding out the top in ragged peaks, oozing red blood. The other individual was nowhere to be found.

He heard a motor running and wanted to stand up, but he'd been injured. Trying to put his weight on his leg, the pain was excruciating, and he passed out like a pussy.

CHAPTER 18

G REG DROPPED KAITLYN off at the crab shack. "Do
you mind bringing her home?" he asked. "I don't
want her driving now."

"Don't you know? When you get pregnant, you
forget how to do everything!" Kaitlyn said, trying to get
her big ass up on one of the stools.

"Please, Martel. It would mean a lot to me," he
begged, even putting his hands together.

"No problem. We'll not be long. I'm tired." Greg
gave her a peck on the cheek, then kissed his wife, and
left.

"I'm sorry, sweetie, I know you were looking forward to that margarita, and now I've just spoiled it."

She couldn't tell her best friend that, as of today,
she wouldn't be doing any more drinking until she
knew the results of a blood test she'd had on the way
home from breakfast with Mr. Karmody.

"No worries, Kate. I'm not really in the mood anyway." She sighed and gulped down half of the oversized glass of ice water. One thing she hadn't gotten used to was the slight sulfur taste of the Florida water. It almost made her gag.

Kaitlyn watched her, the curious grin crossing her pink cheeks. Her eyes sparkled as if she was going to hear some really good gossip. Martel didn't know where to start.

"You can't tell anyone, not even Greg."

At first, Kaitlyn angled her head, frowning. "Oh dear. That bad?"

"It could be." She felt the hot tears collecting in her lower lids. She tried to will them to stop, but it was no use, and she gasped into an ugly, snorting cry that turned heads.

If she noticed, Kaitlyn paid no attention to the reaction of the crowd. She reached across the table and seized Martel's hand. "Your fingers are ice cold. What is going on with you?"

She halfway decided to break her own rules and have a margarita anyway, but she held firm.

Just where do I begin?

As usual, Kate wasn't going to pry. She was going to wait until Martel was collected and wanted to share. She massaged her knuckles and gave her an adoring look, like some of her students did.

"I have a girl in my glass who appears to have been

involved in some sexual activity. And it's spilled over onto the class. She's using her new-found experience, kind of flaunting it in front of a couple of the boys in my class. And, well, I caught her and two boys out behind the field house being inappropriate."

Kate's eyes narrowed as she bored into Martel's stare. "How inappropriate?"

"She let them put their hands down her pants, you know, touch her there. I guess she wanted to impress them or something. She was acting out something she'd been taught and not by another child. Probably an adult. That's the way it works."

"Yes, I know. So you reported it?"

"I reported it to Carlton Green, and we discussed having a parent-teacher conference with the girl's parents before I called the authorities. That way they'd have some kind of idea what they could expect. I didn't want them blindsided by all of it, and, well, frankly, I was also checking out their reaction in case I would have to also report that I thought they were involved."

"Oh. My. God," she said, putting her hand over her mouth. "And are they?"

"I don't know, Kate. My gut tells me no."

"So this is what Green was doing on Monday, meeting with you and the representatives of the child?"

"They obtained a lawyer. They're saying that I didn't keep their daughter safe. That somehow, I'm to blame, that I allowed the boys to abuse her and didn't stop it."

"That's nuts. Someone got to them. So what does Green say?"

"He's kinda wishy-washy. It's like he doesn't want the controversy to come up in the first place. I get the impression that if someone's going to fall over this, it won't be him."

"Have you called your union rep?"

"Three times. No answer."

"You poor thing. So you're in this alone? Well, with Damon being gone, I guess you are. What can I do to help?"

"Nothing. I've hired my own attorney. He thinks it would help if we could identify who the real perpetrator is. So we're maybe hiring a private detective."

"Ouch. That's going to be expensive, isn't it?"

"Lucky thing I was saving up for the wedding."

"No, you can't do that. You can't sacrifice your wedding, Martel. That's just wrong."

"But with this hanging over my head, without it being resolved, how will I ever get a good job in a decent school, either here or in California? And there's the cost. I don't even want to know what Damon will say about all this."

"Oh, he loves you. Don't worry about that."

"He's away on deployment. I told you where."

Kate nodded.

"It's supposed to be very stressful. Oddly enough, they are investigating some sex trafficking cartels there. Very lucrative business helping people cross the border, charging an arm and a leg, and the cartels make them work it off in various terrible ways. Even children."

"I've heard. It's terrible. So rampant now."

"I've told you more than I'm supposed to, about both Damon's work and my situation. If I get sued, I could lose my job and my ability to get another job. The financial setback would be horrible, but worst of all, what kind of an introduction would that have to Ainsley? How would she ever believe in me?"

"Love finds a way, Martel. You know this."

"I've lost those rose-colored glasses, Kate. I really have. I used to be such a Pollyanna about things, always believing the best in people, always believing the best things happen to good people. Here, I thought I was helping them, I wanted them to know about their daughter so she can get some counseling. But it's blown up into a legal affair where it has to be someone else's fault. And it is, truth be told, just that I'm not that someone."

The waitress had come by several times, and neither of them had even looked at the menu.

"I don't think we're very hungry," Kaitlyn said to

the woman.

"Suit yourself, but it's going to get crowded tonight. If I need the table, I'm going to have to ask you to leave."

"How about two bowls of soup? You have some chowder and French bread?" asked Martel.

"Cup or bowl?"

"Bowls." Kate nodded her agreement.

"Coming right up." She took the menus and hustled away to wait on someone else.

"Have you told Damon yet?"

"He knows something's up. But it wasn't until this morning that I found out how much it was going to cost me. He won't be pleased, but I do think we'll have to put the wedding on hold or just do a barn dance or something very easy and inexpensive."

"That actually sounds more like his style, anyway."

"He was letting me do the beach wedding, but no, it wasn't his idea. I just wanted a perfect wedding, like yours."

"It was perfect, wasn't it? But that's because you were there, Martel. You and the kids from the school. That was so cute. Now they're getting into the baby and everything. It's really sweet how all of this is unfolding."

Martel was happy for her, but their two lives didn't have any resemblance of each other. Kaitlyn did everything perfectly. She had the fairy tale wedding with the handsome prince. She had the love and support of the whole school. All the other teachers loved her. The children adored her, and parents tried to get their kids in her class.

Martel was loved and considered a good teacher, but she didn't have that level of respect. Her life was lived under a little rain cloud. She'd given up Ainsley and missed out on ten good years with Damon because she hadn't fought hard enough for them. It was a mistake to take such a passive role in all that. Now there was so much to regret.

All based on the decisions she'd made when she was young. It had changed the whole trajectory of her life.

They hardly spoke all the way to Kate's house. Greg came out and helped her get out of the car, her belly becoming a real obstacle now. Martel remembered those days, when she'd take long walks in the woods and talk to her baby. She told her all about their family, even though she'd never get to meet them. She taught her to listen to the birds and to smell the leaves after it rained, as it always did in Oregon. She'd sit in her car with the windows open looking at the rough surf. An angry surf. Not like Sunset Beach. It was dangerous and relentless, powerful and strong. It made her feel strong as she carried the child she knew was not going to be part of her life. She willed that her daughter would be just as strong but make better choices.

Yes, Ainsley might be one of those, like Kaitlyn, who would have everything, the fairy tale all the way through. She hoped she would learn to appreciate all her gifts and celebrate her life like Martel had.

And someday, maybe she'd forgive her.

She didn't have any reason to expect it but all the reasons in the world to hope it would happen.

CHAPTER 19

D AMON WOKE UP in a hospital bed. He was confused at first, but then the last painful memories of the Mexico trip came flashing by—the explosion, the carnage, even the bizarre celebration of the Day of the Dead when everyone dressed up in skulls, sugar skulls. They worshiped ten-foot-high ghosts and horned creatures who cavorted with the living and coaxed them into their deaths. He'd had all those vivid dreams, but now he was back, amongst the living.

Someone had brought some flowers by, which was nice. Several of the SEAL kids drew pictures. He examined them carefully, pulling himself up on the bar strung across the bed. What caught his eye first was that someone had drawn him on crutches.

He flipped the sheets over and felt the warm bandage covering his upper thigh. He'd either broken his upper femur or his hip. Either one was bad. He guessed it was his hip.

Next to the flowers, one of his brothers brought him some Jack Daniels. He wouldn't mind a drink right now, but he was still on an I.V., and he hadn't been shown how to walk. He didn't want to risk crashing to the floor and maybe breaking his other one.

He lay back, realizing it was exhausting just sitting up. How long had he been there? He must have been unconscious all the way home, because he didn't remember any of it. He did remember the general's boots with parts of his legs sticking out the top, green-stick fractures that would never heal, even if they could find the rest of his body.

Then he remembered the dog. How warm and almost protective that animal was, as he was lunging for his neck. He touched his neck and felt a bruise there. But nothing like what would have occurred if that dog had survived. He hadn't even gotten far enough to break the skin.

"Well, look at what we have here. Mr. Hamlin is up and awake. Is he hungry this morning?"

For some reason, he didn't understand why she was talking that way. Was there someone else in here too? He turned around and, no, just saw the wall with all the monitors on it. He was alone with the nurse. He didn't find her attractive or cute at all. He wanted to throw something at her because she was too pert, too happy, happy, happy. Didn't she know he'd almost died?

His ears still rang too. He tried to talk, and his tongue curled over on itself until he relaxed and tried again, with the same result. It was the strangest thing.

"You're having a reaction to the anesthetic from the surgery to give you a new hip."

"New hip?"

"You've got a brand-new beautiful hip with a titanium ball and new ball socket. And the doctor says you were lucky. It could have been both hips or the injury could have been higher and then you might not have survived."

"Higher?" He couldn't remember any of it.

"Your memory will come back in no time. Some people sleep for days after a trauma like this. Do you remember what hit you?"

"A fuckin' door. A huge solid metal door about as long as this room and five times thicker."

"A flying door. I'll bet that will be an interesting story over beers at the Scupper. You'll have some tall tales like all the other guys there."

"I blew up a general, a Mexican general, too."

"Well, I'm sure you didn't mean it. You should say a prayer for his soul, may he rest in peace."

"No way. I want him to rot in Hell. He was a bad dude." Damon was feeling punchy and then realized she'd put something into the plastic tube that went right into the back of his hand. "Hey, that's not very—

he wanted me to marry his daughter so I blew him up. But I already got a girl—I got two girls, as a matter of fact—"

And then the darkness consumed him.

THE NEXT TIME he woke up he had a splitting headache, more like a migraine. He didn't dare move a muscle, even opening his eyes would risk a blinding flash of yellow light and a pain so great he'd nearly poked his eyes out once to be rid of it.

A rough hand peeled up his eyelid and peered down at him. "Hello, Damon," said Coop.

"Don't touch me. I have a headache."

"Not to worry. Sex is the furthest thing from my mind. Besides your hairy ass is just too, well, it's just too hairy. It doesn't turn me on at all."

Through the foggy dreams with all the bouncing sugar skulls, pictures of little children with their teeth filed to points and blood dripping down their chests haunted him. Just who was he messing around with his eyes, his chart, even making notes in it.

"Hey, that's *my* chart. It's for my doctor, and besides, you're no doctor."

"Why yes, it is. And no, I'm not a doctor. I'm the one who stopped the bleeding so you had a chance to live and hassle all the staff here and be an asshole to me. Your guardian angel. I'm the one who saved your life."

"And I'm the one who blew up a general, and don't you forget it."

"No, I'll never forget that as long as I live. Did you see his boots? They were still shiny."

"I know!" Damon was beginning to warm back up to Coop. Maybe it was the drugs making him think the medic was being a dickhead.

"How did my hip get broken?"

"You mean, how did you manage to blow yourself up and at the last-minute grab a dog to save your sorry life?"

"What was it that happened?"

"The rod that went through the dog went right into your hip and sheared off the top of it. If it had been a few inches up and over toward the middle, and if you hadn't been so freakin scared and shriveled, you might not be able to father any children. But you can breathe a sigh of relief. You can breed to your heart's content. You're checked out. You're fine."

"You handled my junk?"

Coop stood next to the bed with his arms folded. "Nah. I didn't. But I think they would have said something if you were missing anything else."

"Did everyone make it out alive?"

That made Coop sit on the bed and give him a serious look. "We lost Special Agent Ridgeway. But he was half-dead when we found him anyhow. Kelly made it, though. Everyone else made it out in good shape, without a scratch.

"And I bagged a general."

"You bagged a general and a capo. An up-and-coming capo. The head of the Guittierez family in Baja. You rid the planet of a couple of real bad dudes."

"Hey, thanks, man. I'm sorry if I said some scary stuff a few minutes ago. I've had some very weird dreams."

"Damon, you earned your spot on this one. Kyle, everyone is pleased. He's going to come talk to you. But my man, that's one helluva wound and repair. Your days jumping out of airplanes might be over."

"That's bullshit and you know it."

"Ain't up to me. Up to the Navy doctors."

"I want to stay a SEAL. I'm not ready to get out. Don't you let them talk about it like that. You tell them—all of them—I'm staying. I will haunt all you guys down at the SEAL Team 3 building every day and make your lives so miserable you'll wish I died in the explosion."

"Even SEALs have paperwork to do. You can still do that. You could go be an instructor and laugh at froglets and tadpoles and try to get them all to quit. Somebody actually did that once. You could be that guy. I could see it."

"The whole class quit?"

"Yessir. He got relegated to making welcome packets for SEAL graduations, you know, the little programs for the families?"

"And that's where they want to put me. A war hero. A man who sacrificed his hip for the cause, for his brothers."

"Yes, and for blowing up a dog and a general and others. They first give you the medals, and then they give you the desk and the paperwork. You'll see, it isn't that bad."

"Hell no!" Damon shouted.

Coop just laughed at him. "Yeah, that's what I told Kyle. There was no way that was going to happen."

And then he left.

He heard his phone ring and nearly fell out of bed looking for it. When the orderly brought him his tray of food, he asked them to find his phone. He had been sitting on it, but because of the painkillers in his system, his butt didn't feel the vibration.

It had been Martel!

The food smelled divine, but Martel came first.

"Oh God, Damon, they said you broke your hip. I wish I could just fly out there and be with you, sweetheart. Are you in any pain? How did you break your hip? Did anyone else get hurt? Was it an accident?"

"Wait a minute, Martel. I can't think that fast right

now. They've got me so high I'm having nightmares, seeing skeletons and little children with filed teeth. But the long and the short of it is I blew myself up."

He sensed she was confused as to what to say. But then she slowly let out the question, "How did you manage to do that?"

"Well, Fredo showed me what to do. Our timing was off. I was in the process of being eaten by a dog or something. But I was pinned under this monster, and that's what saved my life. Seriously."

"Oh wow. You're really out of it, Damon. So you're not in any pain, then?"

"Not much. I'm about to have my first meal, though." He lifted the white plastic lid. "And it's *mystery meat!* Mashed potatoes and some peas and carrots. I have chocolate pudding for dessert."

She giggled. How he loved to hear her giggle.

"Well, *bon appetite!* Maybe I should call back later?"

"Can you come out? That would be great if you could. I haven't seen you in so long."

"Damon, I was just out there not more than a week ago."

"Yeah, but that's too long. You should just move out here, forget the school. None of this transition bullshit. I want to live with you, Martel. I don't want you clear across the country. What made us think that was a good idea?"

"But I always had this fantasy of getting married at the beach at sunset. Everyone being there. But I'm afraid we'll have to scale back our plans a little."

"Oh? Something else happen?"

"I'll tell you later. Right now, why don't you enjoy your mystery meat, and let's figure it out. Maybe you could come out and stay with me a few months so I can say good-bye."

"Good-bye to whom?"

"Kaitlyn, the beach, the ocean, the vibe of it all."

"Martel, that's nuts. You don't say good-bye to oceans or beaches. Those are inanimate objects. And as for Kaitlyn, she can get on a plane and come visit, or you can go out there and visit. You're not saying good-bye. You're saying hello to San Diego, to me, to the Brotherhood here, to the new school and job I'm sure you'll get. You have a lot to look forward to, but your life is here with me. I don't want to do this any other way."

He must have touched the hang-up button, because when he waited for her answer, there wasn't anyone there.

CHAPTER 20

MARTEL TOOK THE luxury of sleeping in late. At nearly ten o'clock, she finally peeled herself out of bed and made it to the shower. The nausea in the mornings was getting worse and worse, and she knew it would continue until the third month when, miraculously, she'd start to feel full of energy. Or at least that's what had happened the first time.

The pregnancy test came back positive. She didn't want to tell Damon until they could meet in person, and right now, that was looking not for a week or more. He had to learn how to walk up stairs, get in and out of a car by himself, and how to maneuver with a cane as his protection.

And he was in physical therapy three days a week. The progress he was making was very good, he'd told her. She knew how critical to his healing it was to continue that.

He pressed her several times about the wedding

plans, and she withheld that from him as well, figuring it would make more sense after she told him they were going to have another child. She didn't like keeping secrets, but without their face-to-face meetings, it was better this way. And, if he couldn't visit within the next two weeks, well then, she'd tell him. That was the agreement she'd made with herself.

Her administrator let her know that the Gibbs had withdrawn Cora from the school. He quizzed her on what their thoughts might be in regard to them filing a lawsuit, and she told him the absolute truth. She knew nothing. They'd discussed her leaving early, and she offered, if that was what he wanted. But he didn't seem to be pushing her in that direction, so she planned on going back to class on Monday. Her sub had been a student teacher under her two years ago, so she was able to keep up with the class progress.

Once dressed, she made some non-caffeinated tea and was going to go sit out at the beach when she heard the mailman open the creaky box and deposit something. So she picked up the envelopes, sat on the couch overlooking the wide swath of beach, and opened them one by one.

There were a couple of bills, a bank statement, and a letter written by perhaps one of her students. Upon close examination, she discovered it had been post-marked from Palo Alto. All of a sudden, Martel's hands began to shake, and her breathing became shallow.

Ainsley had put a daisy sticker on the back flap of the brown envelope. Martel had not heard anything since that day when they'd met, but the more days that went by left her hopeful. She knew if the decision had been made that Ainsley wanted nothing to do with her or Damon, Mrs. Bergman would have called and stated it so.

The flap gave way, and Martel pulled out a letter on brown matching paper, along with a picture of Ainsley accepting an award for Most Valuable Player for her junior high school basketball team.

She knew Damon would be delighted.

Dear Ms. Long,

I wanted to apologize for my behavior when we met last month. I've talked a lot about it with my parents, and we agreed that I should perhaps make another effort to talk to you again. I really didn't want to, at first, but Mom suggested it when I kept bringing up our meeting. Something had bothered me about that meeting. I still don't know why, but I found myself getting angrier and angrier with you. I'm not angry that you placed me with my parents. It was something else. I'm writing this letter because I didn't want you to think you did something wrong.

I have spring break coming up in two weeks,

and our school will be closed for a week. I was wondering if I might come out to Florida with my mom and visit you. I've seen all these pictures about the beach, and it looks pretty. I've never been to Florida.

Don't feel like you have to say yes to this. I won't be mad. I know you'll be busy teaching, but it would be nice to see where you're going to marry Damon, and maybe I could help with addressing the envelopes or something. If he came out to visit, maybe I could meet him too.

I'm making a wedding present for you guys. It isn't much, but I hope you'll like it.

My mom wanted to know if there were any good motels nearby, not anything fancy, but maybe something within walking distance.

And she says you can call her if you want to meet again. I understand you are probably busy, so I won't expect you'll say yes, but just know that I enjoyed meeting you and would like to get to know you better.

Your friend,
Ainsley.

By the time she got to the end, Martel had lost it. She was having a good, warm but very ugly cry again. Ainsley'd signed the letter "your friend" which touched her greatly. She imagined that Ainsley had struggled with how to close the letter, and that had come to mind after agonizing over it for some time. When she signed her name, she used daisies for the dotted "I" letter, and the "y" was followed by switchbacks with curlicues everywhere, even adding hearts and flowers.

She checked her clock and discovered it was a little before eight in California. Ainsley would be on her way to school or at school soon. Maybe this would be a good time to talk to Lori Newberg.

She dialed her number and got her voicemail.

"Hey, Lori, I just got Ainsley's lovely letter, and I was delighted to hear she was interested in coming out to Florida for a visit. I would be most honored and delighted to put you up in my house. It's very small and not very fancy, but it's right on the beach, and the price is right. I don't have a second bedroom, but I have a very comfortable leather couch in the living room that makes into a sleeper. And you two are welcome to use my bedroom if you want privacy.

"Hope you are doing well, and thanks so much for the letter. You can tell her it meant a lot to me. Hope you guys can come but let me know either way. Take care, Martel."

She'd agreed to meet with Aimee today, so she locked up the house and walked down the beach until she came to their backyard with the gazebo and hot tub facing the gulf. Knocking on the kitchen door, she heard pleasant music from the inside.

"Hey, Martel!" Aimee was dressed in an old shirt of Andy's, which was smudged with paint. She slipped it off and threw it over a chair, inviting her inside. Their large and friendly Golden Retriever tried to pry her way between the two of them. She sat on Martel's feet, begging for pets.

"This is Sandy. She has to be involved in everything now. Notice she helps me paint," Aimee pointed out several places where the dog had gotten too close to a freshly painted off-white surface.

"So what are you painting now? Which room?"

"One of the bedrooms upstairs. We're trying to finish it as a guest room but to double as an office. I've decided to start trying my hand at writing."

"Really?"

"Come see."

She held Sandy's collar while she closed the door behind them. Martel followed her upstairs. The room had access to the balcony overlooking the gulf. On two sides of the room were built in bookshelves, which Aimee had just finished painting. There was an old oak desk facing out, taking up space on the stationary side of the sliding glass door. In the middle of the desk was a blue IBM Selectric typewriter.

"This belonged to Hank Borges, the science fiction

writer who wrote many books right here in this very house, except he used the dining room as his office. This is where he and Carmen fell in love. And guess what, she wrote books after his death."

"Carmen is the lady who left the house to you?"

"Not exactly. I bought it, but yes, she left her estate to me. So, in a way, I got the house money back. It feels like a never-ending circle, doesn't it?"

"Something. Definitely something. Is it in the air, or is it the house? Or maybe a ghost!"

"I know. I felt it the first time I came in here. I don't think it's a ghost. It's just a very creative vortex or something. I don't want to study it too much for fear of scaring it away."

"It is a spirit then. That's how you see it?" Martel asked.

"No, I don't see it. I *feel* it. I sit down at the type-writer, feel the keys underneath my fingers, and something just connects. It's almost like I can't stop."

"What are you writing?"

"Novels about falling in love at the beach. You know, the fairy tale everyone wants but no one really gets?"

"Some people do, I think." Martel was recalling the conversation she'd had with herself about Kaitlyn.

"Anyway, it's very healing here. Something about these four walls is healing to me. I feel like creating. I've heard about houses like this. There are several in

England, famous writers and poets lived in them, passed them down from one to another, a solid chain of creativity through hundreds of years. I think I've found one here. It was dormant, and then one day, Carmen stepped inside, and it transformed Hank's life."

Martel watched Aimee, grinning.

"You don't believe me, do you?"

"No, I do. I've just never experienced it before. I'm happy for you."

"Oh, all right. I'm boring you, aren't I?"

"Not at all."

Sandy sat next to where Martel was standing, leaning into her. She brushed the top of the golden dog's head. The room was lit from the large window but seemed to have another glow all its own, too.

"You like this room, Sandy?" she said to the dog, who looked back adoringly at her.

"She likes to sit by the window and watch people walk on the beach. When she's left alone, she always comes here."

They went downstairs, where Aimee had prepared a green salad for both of them. "You want some coffee or wine?" she asked.

"No, thanks. Water would be great."

"So how are the wedding plans coming. You reserved the gazebo at Sunset Beach?"

"I did. But something's come up, and I think I'm going to let it go."

"Oh dear. What happened?"

"I'm not at liberty to talk about it, but I've run into some extra expenses, and me without a job for next year, I just thought it would be good to cut back. Besides, Damon hasn't really been sending out the invitations, so it's kind of stupid to spend a lot of money on a party where not many people will come."

"You could use it to help purchase something back in Coronado when you move there."

"Exactly. I just re-thought the expense of it." She didn't want to lie to her friend, but there was no safe way of letting her know.

"I offered to let you use this house for your reception. I don't see why you couldn't get married out here at the beach and have the reception here. We did it. It was perfect. The offer still stands."

"Are you sure?"

"Of course. I'll even have it catered. Let me do that for the two of you."

"I couldn't ask you to do that. That's way over the top."

"Nonsense. If you have it catered, it won't drive you crazy with all the work. They come in, prepare, then clean up, and you're left with a beautiful house with wonderful memories. You don't have to spend a week to clean up after, either. Seriously, it's the only way to go."

"Well then, I accept. On one condition."

"Sure, what?"

"I want Damon's approval first."

"He's coming out here?"

"He is. In about two weeks." She didn't want to discuss Ainsley's possible visit yet so left it at that.

"I'm so excited. I hope he likes it."

MARTEL LEFT AIMEE'S house feeling very light and hopeful. On the way back to her place, she got a call from her attorney.

"Our private investigator has come up with some past arrest records for Mrs. Gibbs' father and two uncles. They all center around child sexual abuse. Unfortunately, it goes back generations. It's heartbreaking. She probably grew up in it and was a victim herself."

"It fits the pattern, doesn't it?" Martel said. "I feel so sorry for those kids in that family."

"We have some choices, so I need to know. You could report your suspicions. Child Protective Services will have to investigate, but it could hit the paper and get lots of publicity."

"Is that what you'd do?"

"I would."

"I think I want that too. Main thing is to get Cora some help. The whole family is going to need help."

"Always a possibility when it hits the paper, they'll

mention how the investigation started. I just want you to be okay with the extra scrutiny."

"I want what's good for Cora. This isn't for me. It's for Cora."

"Brave little lady, if you ask me. I'll email you some of the investigator's findings, the arrest records, which are public record, but you have to know the dates and things to put them on the trail. There are several unsolved cases, too. We'd be helping the sheriff's department."

"Let's do it. I'm driving home right now. So does that solve the potential lawsuit with their attorney?"

"Only a matter of days now. I think you're almost in the clear."

"That's the best news I've had in a long time. Thank you so much."

"Not quite out of the woods yet but nearing the clearing, as we say. Don't forget to make that call."

"Nothing could tear me away from that mission. Thanks once again."

Her phone pinged, and she read the text message from Damon.

'Got approval for early release and leave. When should I come?'

She didn't have to think more than five seconds. She texted him back, *'How about tomorrow?'*

CHAPTER 21

Two Weeks Later

DAMON CHANGED HIS clothes three times before they left for the Tampa Airport, each time fussing with his balance, using the cane he'd been told to use to help support his new hip.

"You're fine. Don't keep doing that, Damon. She's not going to notice any of this," Martel insisted. "I don't want you to hurt yourself."

He'd started with khakis then some long Chinos, the relaxed fit jeans. His canvas slip-ons would go with either of these. He opted for a clean white button-down long-sleeved shirt. While Martel put away the two pairs of pants he didn't wear, he sorted through the three jackets he had, deciding on the dark grey one.

"Come on. Honestly, Damon, you're worse than any of my girlfriends ever were. As long as you smell good and don't look all wild and scary, she's going to like you just fine."

"Do I smell good? Tell me honestly."

She approached, delicately pulling his shirt toward her. Her forefinger ran across his lower lip as she leaned into him and kissed him. It was natural to wrap his arms around her, pull her into his chest, and feel all the wonderful ways she filled all the vacant and painful parts of him. How could he have ever let her go? he wondered. What a complete idiot to have missed all those years. But she was here now, and he was going to make sure she never got away again.

His body responded with the delicious slow arousal that always had been there, from the first time he'd ever kissed her. With how she showed she needed him like tugging on the top button of his shirt or the way her fingers traced the arch of his ear or the satisfied look on her sweet face when she shattered beneath him, Martel always brought her A game. The more he spent time with her the more he couldn't live without her.

"I asked you if I smelled okay," he said between kisses.

"I'm thinking about it," her soft pink lips purred. She inhaled and her eyelids fluttered just a bit. "Oh my. I'm wet, Damon."

"That happens when you're pregnant too?"

"Why wouldn't it? I feel it. Why wouldn't I get ready for you? All those pheromones, all those ancient mating rituals through time that we're part of."

"So is it worth it to be late?"

"Maybe just a quickie, if you can."

"I can do it anyway you like it, sweetheart."

She had her clothes off within seconds. He removed his for the fourth time, knelt, and kissed her belly button.

"Now I get to have all this, to watch you grow, Martel. This time I get to have everythin."

He kissed her again there. "Thank you. Thank you bringing me this gift."

She lazily sorted through the top of his head as he stroked her wetness.

"I wish we had more time," she sighed.

"Honey, we got all the time in the world."

She turned to present her rear to him, and he slipped inside smoothly, feeling the early fullness in her breasts, one hand gently placed on her abdomen as he stroked her carefully, kissed her neck, and felt the ripple of her spine triggering his own arousal.

"I can never get enough, Martel. I never could. I still can't."

Her muscles contracted and fluttered. She reached behind, pulled her butt cheeks apart, and gave him deeper access, and he took every bit she would give him. "I can't wait to fuck you when you're huge."

"I get horny when I'm pregnant. I want it all the

time, Damon," she whispered.

"Music to my ears, sweetheart. I'm going to make sure I'm here for you every time you want it."

Their quick interlude was over too soon but lingered still as he helped her get dressed and they drove to the airport, holding hands and kissing as he helped her out of the car and placed his palm on her ass and rubbed. It was divine being in love with her, made even more special by the fact that she was carrying his child. Again.

Not everything was settled with Martel's school situation, but with the potential lawsuit dropped, and the arrest of the mother's relatives, charged also with Cora's abuse, he could see some of her excitement for teaching and for the remainder of her school year coming back. Her teaching was as important to her as his being on the SEAL team. And, as long as he healed properly, and didn't get given a medical, they'd both be able to do what they loved to do, and do it in San Diego.

He'd stopped to buy some flowers this morning. As they stood in the lobby area waiting for the passengers to arrive on their way to baggage claim, he held those flowers, a spring bouquet with apricot daffodils.

As Martel greeted Mrs. Newberg, Damon saw Ainsley—her face almost like looking into a mirror and seeing his own face there. She was embarrassed, too, looked down at the flowers and then back at him, smiling, happy, tall, and strong. She was a beautiful young woman who was only going to be more beautiful as the years descended upon her. He extended his hand, and she took the flowers he offered. His heart beat so loud surely they all could hear it.

"And here you are. I get to meet you at last. I'm so proud, Ainsley. Thank you for agreeing to meet me."

"Of course," she said with a shrug, except she didn't convince him that she was casual about it. He felt it was as heartfelt for her as it was for him. She would always be a miracle to him, and he'd remember this day for the rest of his life.

Martel and Lori Newberg smugly smiled between themselves, having shared something he wasn't privy to.

How could he be so lucky that he could get to know this beautiful young lady with poise and grace, her long blonde hair like spun gold, with the clearest blue eyes he'd ever seen. He was completely enamored by her.

"Damon, this is Lori Newberg, Ainsley's mom."

Yes, she is her mother. "Thank you and so lovely to meet you."

"You're not at all like what I thought you'd be," she said.

"I know, you thought I'd be a big wild guy with tats all over his body and scars on his face or something?"

She giggled. "Something like that." She looked at Ainsley. "Right?"

"He does sort of look like Dad. Wait until you meet him. You'll get along with him, I know," she said.

Damon still couldn't take his eyes off her. "I'm speechless. I really am," he said.

"We'd better get downstairs and get their luggage before they put it in the lost and found, Damon. Can I peel you away for just a few more minutes until we gather everything up?"

"Of course. Here, let me take those," he said as he reached for her backpack and Lori's carryon bag.

"We're good. Help us with the heavy stuff," Lori Newberg said.

Downstairs at the claim, their bags were making their way around the carousel. Ainsley pointed out their luggage, and Damon retrieved them both, grabbed his cane and they headed for the short-term garage.

He listened to the ladies' happy banter, enjoying being in their presence. In just under an hour, they were turning off the freeway toward the beaches.

"Look at all that blue water, Mom. And all the boats!" Ainsley said.

"Really gorgeous. I can understand why you like it so much."

"I fell in love with this place the instant I took my

first look at the Gulf and the white sand beach. I'm going to miss it, but I have so many happy memories here," Martel said.

He looked at her animated face. "And now you're about to make more memories, sweetheart." She smiled back at him.

At the house, all four of them stared through the sliding glass door onto the beach and glittering bay beyond.

"Come on, Ainsley, take a walk with me," he said to her.

"Okay. Mom, you want to come?"

"No, you go ahead. Take a walk with Damon. I'll stay here and get our things settled."

Damon observed her long gait as they headed down the beach toward the hard sand and the surf beyond. "We often do this at sunset. Wait until you see that. Really magical."

"There's no one here. I expected it to be crowded from all the news reports I've seen."

"A well-kept secret, my dear. Not everywhere looks like Miami. We like this sleepy little coastal community. The pace isn't too fast. It's quaint, in a way. All the normal people are here. That's what I keep telling Martel all the time."

"I always wanted to know what you thought when you first found out about me."

"I saw these pictures of Martel, month by month, and I couldn't believe it. I thought she'd had a baby with someone else, to be honest. She sat down and she told me, and then she showed me your picture in your school basketball uniform." Damon stopped. "It was a miracle, Ainsley. I couldn't believe it."

She liked that, Damon noted.

"What did you think when your parents told you about the adoption?"

"I didn't believe it at first. But then they explained that they chose me, that I was special. I always felt special."

"You are special."

"But they made sure every day was special for me."

"You're one lucky little girl. You have lots of people who love you, Ainsley."

"It's nice to finally get to meet you. And Mom says you're going to have another child?"

"We are. You'll be a big sister."

"Are you totally okay with all this? I mean, I'm going to still call them my parents, because they are. Does that make you feel bad?"

Damon smiled back. "Do I wish I'd done things differently? Yes. I think everyone always knows when they could have done things better. But the main thing is that we're all together now. And I get such enjoyment just being able to share a little piece of you.

Thank you, Ainsley. I'll always be here for you. I'm never going away again."

Did you enjoy reading Second Chance Reunion? Stay tuned for the next two books in the Sunset SEALs series, releasing later this year. Stay connected by signing up for Sharon's newsletter here so you won't miss the next installment of Sunset SEALs.

authorsharonhamilton.com/contact

If you'd like to start reading Sharon's SEAL books from the very beginning, you can start with Accidental SEAL, which is the book that launched the whole series.

Here's a detailed listing of all Sharon's books, by series:

SEAL BOOKS

SEAL BROTHERHOOD SERIES

Accidental SEAL Book 1

Fallen SEAL Legacy Book 2

SEAL Under Covers Book 3

SEAL The Deal Book 4

Cruisin' For A SEAL Book 5

SEAL My Destiny Book 6

SEAL of My Heart Book 7

Fredo's Dream Book 8

SEAL My Love Book 9

SEAL Encounter Prequel to Book 1

SEAL Endeavor Prequel to Book 2

Ultimate SEAL Collection Vol. 1 Books 1-4 /2 Prequels

Ultimate SEAL Collection Vol. 2 Books 5-7

SEAL BROTHERHOOD LEGACY SERIES

Watery Grave Book 1

BAD BOYS OF SEAL TEAM 3 SERIES

SEAL's Promise Book 1

SEAL My Home Book 2

SEAL's Code Book 3

Big Bad Boys Bundle Books 1-3

BAND OF BACHELORS SERIES

Lucas Book 1

Alex Book 2

Jake Book 3

Jake 2 Book 4

Big Band of Bachelors Bundle

BONE FROG BROTHERHOOD SERIES

New Year's SEAL Dream Book 1

SEALed At The Altar Book 2

SEALed Forever Book 3

SEAL's Rescue Book 4

SEALed Protection Book 5

BONE FROG BACHELOR SERIES
Bone Frog Bachelor Book 0.5
Unleashed Book 1

SUNSET SEALS SERIES
SEALed at Sunset Book 1
Second Chance SEAL Book 2
Treasure Island SEAL Book 3
Escape to Sunset Book 4
The House at Sunset Beach Book 5
Second Chance Reunion Book 6

LOVE VIXEN
Bone Frog Love

SHADOW SEALS
Shadow of the Heart

SILVER SEALS SERIES
SEAL Love's Legacy

SLEEPER SEALS SERIES
Bachelor SEAL

STAND ALONE BOOKS & SERIES
SEAL's Goal: The Beautiful Game
Nashville SEAL: Jameson
True Blue SEALS Zak
Paradise: In Search of Love

Love Me Tender, Love You Hard

NOVELLAS

SEAL You In My Dreams Magnolias and Moonshine

PARANORMALS

GOLDEN VAMPIRES OF TUSCANY SERIES

Honeymoon Bite Book 1

Mortal Bite Book 2

Christmas Bite Book 3

Midnight Bite Book 4

THE GUARDIANS

Heavenly Lover Book 1

Underworld Lover Book 2

Underworld Queen Book 3

Redemption Book 4

FALL FROM GRACE SERIES

Gideon: Heavenly Fall

NOVELLAS

SEAL Of Time Trident Legacy

All of Sharon's books are available on Audible,
narrated by the talented J.D. Hart.

ABOUT THE AUTHOR

NYT and USA/Today Bestselling Author Sharon Hamilton's SEAL Brotherhood series have earned her author rankings of #1 in Romantic Suspense, Military Romance and Contemporary Romance. Her other *Brotherhood* stand-alone series are: Bad Boys of SEAL Team 3, Band of Bachelors, True Blue SEALs, Nashville SEALs, Bone Frog Brotherhood, Sunset SEALs, Bone Frog Bachelor Series and SEAL Brotherhood Legacy Series. She is a contributing author to the very popular Shadow SEALs multi-author series.

Her SEALs and former SEALs have invested in two wineries, a lavender farm and a brewery in Sonoma County, which have become part of the new stories. They also have expanded to include Veteran-benefit projects on the Florida Gulf Coast, as well as projects in Africa and the Maldives. One of the SEAL wives has even launched her own women's fiction series. But old characters, as well as children of these SEAL heroes keep returning to all the newer books.

Sharon also writes sexy paranormals in two series: Golden Vampires of Tuscany and The Guardians.

A lifelong organic vegetable and flower gardener, Sharon and her husband lived for fifty years in the Wine Country of Northern California, where many of her stories take place. Recently, they have moved to the beautiful Gulf Coast of Florida, with stories of shipwrecks, the white sugar-sand beaches of Sunset, Treasure Island and Indian Rocks Beaches.

She loves hearing from fans through her website: authorsharonhamilton.com

Find out more about Sharon, her upcoming releases, appearances and news when you sign up for Sharon's newsletter.

Facebook:
facebook.com/SharonHamiltonAuthor

Twitter:
twitter.com/sharonlhamilton

Pinterest:
pinterest.com/AuthorSharonH

Amazon:
amazon.com/Sharon-Hamilton/e/B004FQQMAC

BookBub:
bookbub.com/authors/sharon-hamilton

Youtube:

youtube.com/channel/UCDInkxXFpXp_4Vnq08ZxMBQ

Soundcloud:

soundcloud.com/sharon-hamilton-1

Sharon Hamilton's Rockin' Romance Readers:

facebook.com/groups/sealteamromance

Sharon Hamilton's Goodreads Group:

goodreads.com/group/show/199125-sharon-hamilton-readers-group

Visit Sharon's Online Store:

sharon-hamilton-author.myshopify.com

Join Sharon's Review Teams:

eBook Reviews:

sharonhamiltonassistant@gmail.com

Audio Reviews:

sharonhamiltonassistant@gmail.com

Life *is one fool thing after another.*
Love *is two fool things after each other.*

REVIEWS

PRAISE FOR THE
GOLDEN VAMPIRES OF TUSCANY SERIES

"Well to say the least I was thoroughly surprise. I have read many Vampire books, from Ann Rice to Kym Grosso and few other Authors, so yes I do like Vampires, not the super scary ones from the old days, but the new ones are far more interesting far more human than one can remember. I found Honeymoon Bite a totally engrossing book, I was not able to put it down, page after page I found delight, love, understanding, well that is until the bad bad Vamp started being really bad. But seeing someone love another person so much that they would do anything to protect them, well that had me going, then well there was more and for a while I thought it was the end of a beautiful love story that spanned not only time but, spanned Italy and California. Won't divulge how it ended, but I did shed a few tears after screaming but Sharon Hamilton did not let me down, she took me on amazing trip that I loved, look forward to reading another Vampire book of hers."

"An excellent paranormal romance that was exciting, romantic, entertaining and very satisfying to read. It had me anticipating what would happen next many times over, so much so I could not put it down and even finished it up in a day. The vampires in this book were different from your average vampire, but I enjoy different variations and changes to the same old stuff. It made for a more unpredictable read and more adventurous to explore! Vampire lovers, any paranormal readers and even those who love the romance genre will enjoy Honeymoon Bite."

"This is the first non-Seal book of this author's I have read and I loved it. There is a cast-like hierarchy in this vampire community with humans at the very bottom and Golden vampires at the top. Lionel is a dark vampire who are servants of the Goldens. Phoebe is a Golden who has not decided if she will remain human or accept the turning to become a vampire. Either way she and Lionel can never be together since it is forbidden.

I enjoyed this story and I am looking forward to the next installment."

"A hauntingly romantic read. Old love lost and new love found. Family, heart, intrigue and vampires. Grabbed my attention and couldn't put down. Would definitely recommend."

PRAISE FOR THE
SEAL BROTHERHOOD SERIES

"Fans of Navy SEAL romance, I found a new author to feed your addiction. Finely written and loaded delicious with moments, Sharon Hamilton's storytelling satisfies like a thick bar of chocolate." —Marliss Melton, bestselling author of the *Team Twelve* Navy SEALs series

"Sharon Hamilton does an EXCELLENT job of fitting all the characters into a brotherhood of SEALS that may not be real but sure makes you feel that you have entered the circle and security of their world. The stories intertwine with each book before...and each book after and THAT is what makes Sharon Hamilton's SEAL Brotherhood Series so very interesting. You won't want to put down ANY of her books and they will keep you reading into the night when you should be sleeping. Start with this book...and you will not want to stop until you've read the whole series and then...you will be waiting for Sharon to write the next one." (5 Star Review)

"Kyle and Christy explode all over the pages in this first book, *[Accidental SEAL],* in a whole new series of SEALs. If the twist and turns don't get your heart jumping, then maybe the suspense will. This is a must read for those that are looking for love and adventure with a little sloppy love thrown in for good measure." (5 Star Review)

PRAISE FOR THE
BAD BOYS OF SEAL TEAM 3 SERIES

"I love reading this series! Once you start these books, you can hardly put them down. The mix of romance and suspense keeps you turning the pages one right after another! Can't wait until the next book!" (5 Star Review)

"I love all of Sharon's Seal books, but *[SEAL's Code]* may just be her best to date. Danny and Luci's journey is filled with a wonderful insight into the Native American life. It is a love story that will fill you with warmth and contentment. You will enjoy Danny's journey to become a SEAL and his reasons for it. Good job Sharon!" (5 Star Review)

PRAISE FOR THE
BAND OF BACHELORS SERIES

"[Lucas] was the first book in the Band of Bachelors series and it was a phenomenal start. I loved how we got to see the other SEALs we all love and we got a look at Lucas and Marcy. They had an instant attraction, and their love was very intense. This book had it all, suspense, steamy romance, humor, everything you want in a riveting, outstanding read. I can't wait to read the next book in this series." (5 Star Review)

PRAISE FOR THE
TRUE BLUE SEALS SERIES

"Keep the tissues box nearby as you read *True Blue SEALs: Zak* by Sharon Hamilton. I imagine more than I wish to that the circumstances surrounding Zak and Amy are all too real for returning military personnel and their families. Ms. Hamilton has put us right in the middle of struggles and successes that these two high school sweethearts endure. I have read several of Sharon Hamilton's military romances but will say this is the most emotionally intense of the ones that I have read. This is a well-written, realistic story with authentic characters that will have you rooting for them and proud of those who serve to keep us safe. This is an author who writes amazing stories that you love and cry with the characters. Fans of Jessica Scott and Marliss Melton will want to add Sharon Hamilton to their list of realistic military romance writers." (5 Star Review)

"Dear FATHER IN HEAVEN,

If I may respectfully say so sometimes you are a strange God. Though you love all mankind,

It seems you have special predilections too.

You seem to love those men who can stand up alone who face impossible odds, Who challenge every bully and every tyrant ~

Those men who know the heat and loneliness of Calvary. Possibly you cherish men of this stamp because you recognize the mark of your only son in them.

Since this unique group of men known as the SEALs know Calvary and suffering, teach them now the mystery of the resurrection ~ that they are indestructible, that they will live forever because of their deep faith in you.

And when they do come to heaven, may I respectfully warn you, Dear Father, they also know how to celebrate. So please be ready for them when they insert under your pearly gates.

Bless them, their devoted Families and their Country on this glorious occasion.

We ask this through the merits of your Son, Christ Jesus the Lord, Amen."

By Reverend E.J. McMalhon S.J. LCDR, CHC, USN
Awards Ceremony SEAL Team One
1975 At NAB, Coronado

www.ingramcontent.com/pod-product-compliance
Lightning Source LLC
Chambersburg PA
CBHW060151180626
46813CB00007B/2709